JEANMARIE
and the FBI

JEANMARIE
and the FBI

APPLE VALLEY
MYSTERIES

Lucille Travis

Baker Books
A Division of Baker Book House Co
Grand Rapids, Michigan 49516

© 2000 by Lucille Travis

Published by Baker Books
a division of Baker Book House Company
P.O. Box 6287, Grand Rapids, MI 49516-6287

Printed in the United States of America

ISBN 0-8010-4471-5

Library of Congress Cataloging-in-Publication Data is on file at the Library of Congress, Washington, D. C.

For current information about all releases from Baker Book House, visit our web site:
http://www.bakerbooks.com

Contents

Undercover

*A*t 6:00, the official wartime blackout began, and the lights in the small towns near the tip of Long Island, New York, disappeared behind heavy blackout curtains. In the darkness of the night, without moon or stars to guide travelers, had there been any abroad, a sign picturing an American soldier and the words "Your Country Needs You" flapped in the wind. Miles of deserted beach, hidden from the rest of the island by tall sand dunes, lay open to the Atlantic Ocean. Small waves rolling in slapped against rocks, ran onto shore and out again. Not far out something large and shadowy had risen from the cold waters. Silently, a German submarine emerged. Moments later four men climbed from the hatch. Quickly and silently the men loaded supplies into rubber rafts and cast off towards shore. By the time they reached it, the sub had slipped back below the water.

The four went to work swiftly. When they finished, boxes, rubber rafts, all

7

were gone, buried in a deep hole. The leader of the group checked his watch. "Good," he said. "You know the plan. We will meet again at the camp." Without further words the men parted, two to the north of the island, and two heading west in the direction of the road to New York City. It had begun to snow.

In the darkness of the night, deep in the countryside two hours north of New York City, the snow fell quietly, swirling about the Apple Valley Orphanage, piling onto windowsills, and covering rooftops. No one saw the chicken thief with his burlap bag over his shoulder leave the orphanage grounds and head for the deserted Gould's summer camp.

In his small butcher shop a few miles away from the Apple Valley Orphanage, Gustav Schmidt picked up the last of his carefully wrapped packages, turned out the light, and headed for his truck. The light snow of a few hours ago now fell heavily. He thought of his warm house waiting for him, and his supper, but he had promised and must keep his word. The war America was fighting overseas had brought such shortages of meat that many butcher shops were dangerously near to closing. He could not afford to lose his good customers, not now when the government used so much meat for the military that there was a fifty-percent shortage for civilians, even with rationing. He climbed into his truck, let the motor warm, then drove in the direction of Apple Valley. With gas rationing the government had set a thirty-five-mile-per-hour speed limit for all civilians, but tonight it was just as well. Like everyone else he must drive without headlights thanks to the war and blackout restrictions. He would have to drive slowly so he would not miss the orphanage. Its main building and cottages sprawled across several acres of woods and farmland marked by a boundary of low stone walls.

Prologue

The windshield wipers slapped steadily in the silence as Gustav peered into the darkness. He would park on the road near a patch of woods running by the grounds. Fortunately, this storm would hide his truck well. He was glad he had worn thick walking boots for the rest of the way.

ONE

A Strange Meeting

Jeanmarie shivered as she wriggled into her nightgown. The gown, a hand-me-down donated to the orphanage, barely reached below her knees. Its blue flowers looked faded next to the bright red where she'd embroidered her initials, Jm. A heavy gust of wind rattled the window of the small north side room with its five iron cots, and she shivered again.

From across the room Pearl called softly, "We can push our beds together after lights are out and spread the blankets double."

Jeanmarie nodded. Pearl, thin as she was, suffered the worst of all of them from the winter cold. There were no extra blankets. The twins, Tess and Maria, would share their blankets tonight. Jeanmarie glanced at the two who were already busy loosening the blankets from their tightly tucked corners. That left only Winnie. She smiled. With the thick layer of soft old dust rags she and Pearl had pinned to the inside of Winnie's nightgown to pad it, she should be warm enough.

The sudden loud wailing of the Apple Valley Orphanage air-raid siren stifled all conversation.

As it died away into the wind the phone in the hallway rang. Mrs. Foster, the housemother, clattered down the hall to answer it. Her voice carried to the dorm. "Yes, yes. Thank you, Dr. Werner." A moment later she called loudly, "This is a practice drill only, girls. See that the blackout curtains are drawn. Lights out in five minutes."

Jeanmarie took a deep breath. Because of the war they practiced air-raid drills once a month at the orphanage. But ever since Pearl Harbor one never knew when it might be the real thing.

Pearl sat up in bed, her brown eyes wide in her thin, freckled face. "Luke will be coming," she said. "I hope he brings sweet rolls again."

Jeanmarie gave her braids a final twist. One of the older boys, Luke, had air-raid warden duty during practices. His job was to check the orphanage grounds for telltale lights that might lead an enemy plane to its target in a real raid. His first stop was their cottage, Wheelock.

"If he's been working for the bakery, he just might," she said. Last month he had brought them sugared rolls, tossing the bag up in the darkness into the open window where Jeanmarie and the others always waved to him on his rounds. Though Luke lived and worked in the orphanage, now that he was almost eighteen he was hired out for occasional work. The bakery in town often added day-old rolls to his pay.

"As soon as Foster makes her rounds we'll open the window for him," Jeanmarie said as she burrowed under the covers and pulled them up to her chin. The thought of a sweet roll made her stomach rumble. For supper they'd had goulash, a mixture of day-old bread with bits of peppers, tomatoes, onions, and pieces of tough eggplant. "Do you suppose we'll have goulash again tomorrow night?" she said softly. Groans came from the twins' direction as well as Pearl's.

"We should have just eaten it tonight," Winnie said. Her fine blonde hair hung straight, framing her face, and her blue eyes were earnest. Everyone knew Mrs. Foster never wasted anything.

Jeanmarie wriggled her toes to warm them. Sugar and meat and lots of things were rationed because of the war, but the orphanage had its own small farm and raised most of their food. All thoughts of food fled as Mrs. Foster appeared in the doorway.

The housemother's steel-rimmed glasses matched her gray hair swept back tight against her head into a bun at the back of her neck. When she frowned as she did now it made her look stern. "Let's have quiet in here," she said, flicking off the light switch and plunging the room into darkness.

Jeanmarie waited as the housemother's heavy footsteps stopped next at the younger girls' quarters across the hall and then at the foot of the stairs to the attic where the older girls slept. At last her steps retreated down the hall, and the door to Mrs. Foster's private rooms slammed shut.

"That's it," Jeanmarie whispered. She sat up in bed and listened for a moment to be sure. Mrs. Foster had one good habit—back in her own rooms, her work done for the day, she rarely left them. The floor felt icy as Jeanmarie's bare feet touched it, and she hurried toward the window.

Across the room Winnie's thin voice whispered, "Just let me know when Luke comes. I think I'm coming down with a cold."

"Never mind, Win," Pearl called softly. "If Luke brings anything I'll see that you get your share."

Jeanmarie glanced at Pearl. Last winter one of Winnie's colds had turned into flu, and she had nearly died. Before it was over all of them had had it. Quickly Jeanmarie ran to the dresser, felt for her sweater, and threw it across Winnie's bed. "Put it on, Win, and stay under the covers for goodness sake."

Pearl hugged a much-darned wool sweater across her thin chest as she stood by the window waiting.

Pulling back the lower half of the heavy blackout curtain, Jeanmarie peered into the darkness. She slid her fingers along the frame until she felt the metal lock, then pushed it open and eased the window up a few inches. "We can lift it the rest of the way when he gets here," she said.

Pearl drew her hand back from the window ledge. "It's snowing!" she exclaimed. Wet flakes piled in a thin layer on the sill. "Why would Dr. Werner have an air-raid drill when it's snowing?" She brushed a bit of snow from the sill. "Even enemy planes can't fly in snowstorms."

"If Werner wants to hold a practice drill tonight it doesn't have to make sense," Jeanmarie said as she shrugged her shoulders. Dr. Werner was head of the orphanage and ruled as he pleased. A cold gust of wind blew the curtains, and, shivering, Jeanmarie crouched down on her knees so only her head was above the windowsill. Pearl huddled beside her. The twins crowded in next to them. Without a moon it was dark and silent except for the swish of falling snow. Jeanmarie hugged her knees to keep warm. They hadn't yet missed waving Luke on in his rounds even though the cold of winter practices made it harder.

"I see his flashlight!" Pearl whispered. A small but steady beam came toward them from below the hill leading to the orphanage cottages for girls. At the same time a car motor rattled along on the road outside the low stone wall that bordered Wheelock Cottage. The motor idled then stopped.

Jeanmarie sat up straight. It was late at night for a car to be stopping here. Besides that, with gas rationing few cars passed this far out in the country where the orphanage grounds were. As she watched, a second light appeared from the direction of the road. Someone with a flashlight was heading straight up Wheelock's driveway. Any second whoever it was would run right into Luke!

Pearl gripped Jeanmarie's arm. "It must be somebody from town; maybe Luke knows him!"

Luke's light was no more than a few feet from the house when he stopped walking. The figure with the second flashlight kept coming.

In the falling snow and darkness the two flashlights met, looking like small lamps with thousands of white moths swarming around them. Although the two figures were close to the house their faces were hidden outside the circles of light. But the deep voice carrying to the window could never be mistaken. Pearl gasped as Jeanmarie whispered, "Werner!"

Dr. Werner's voice, loud and commanding as a general's, carried through the open window. "You made good time. You have brought the package?" Her hands trembling, Jeanmarie smoothed the heavy air-raid curtain into place over the open window. With her ear against the windowsill just below the curtain's edge she strained to listen.

The next words came from a voice she didn't recognize. "Ja, I have brought vat you need, mein friend. Such veather. Gut for us but bad for . . ." A gust of wind tore away the rest of the words. But she had heard enough to know that the voice with the accent was not Luke's.

Dr. Werner was saying, "You are a good friend to have these days. All of us thank you. I did not want my wife to become suspicious. It's a good German . . ." Again the wind made it impossible for Jeanmarie to hear. Daringly she opened the curtain a crack. The men were leaving. One flashlight had turned back on the driveway toward the road. The second light blinked down the hill away from Wheelock Cottage in the direction of Dr. Werner's house.

Ignoring Pearl's firm tug on her sleeve, Jeanmarie leaned far out of the window and watched both lights disappear. A motor coughed, caught, and chugged away into the night. Jeanmarie's thoughts raced. "Werner isn't even bothering to make the rounds," she whispered.

Back inside the room with the window shut, Jeanmarie felt goosebumps on her arms. She swallowed hard. "What if we'd called out and waved the flashlight thinking it was Luke out there?" she said, thinking out loud.

Pearl groaned softly. "We'd have been in deep trouble, that's what."

Jeanmarie peered through the windowpane into the night. There were no lights now. "No Luke, that's for sure," she said. Seated on her cot the four of them huddled under the blanket. Across the room Winnie snored lightly.

"Whatever was in that package," Jeanmarie said, "Werner wanted it kept secret. He didn't even want his wife to know about it. What we do know is that it was something German."

Tess's dark eyes looked puzzled. "What happened to Luke?" she asked.

"And who was the man with the German accent? That had to be his car we heard," Maria said.

Jeanmarie flicked her flashlight on and muffled its light in her hands as she spoke. "At least we can find out why Luke didn't show up for duty tonight. Tess, you go by the barns on your way to work, right?" In the orphanage everybody worked. Tess mended clothes at the boys' cottages four days a week after school. To get there she had to pass the barns where Luke worked.

In the semidarkness Tess's voice sounded thoughtful. "If nobody is around I'll try to ask him," she said.

Jeanmarie turned to Maria. The twins were alike, dark eyes, dark curly hair, except for the small beauty mark on the left side of Maria's face. "You dust for the Werners on Mondays, right?"

"Yes, and I clean the upstairs hall and bath till they shine." Maria's soft voice was proud.

Jeanmarie nodded. "Good. What we need is a clue about tonight, maybe something Werner wrote down then tossed in a wastebasket. Anything like addresses, letters, or notes might help us figure out what went on tonight."

"Werner's a German name," Pearl said slowly. "And didn't he call the other man a good German?" She sat up, her thin shoulders hunched. "What if our own Dr. Werner is a German agent?"

Jeanmarie started to laugh then stopped. "Werner? We've all called him lots of things like stiff-necked, iron heart," she said, "but an enemy agent?"

"Think about it," Pearl insisted. "Only two weeks ago the newspaper said the FBI arrested four American Germans for helping German prisoners escape. What if Werner is passing on information, documents for the Germans on his trips into the city? You know he goes into the city once a week."

Jeanmarie tried to picture Dr. Werner as an enemy agent. "We know for sure nobody showed up for that practice drill besides Dr. Werner and a stranger," she said. "The whole thing was phony, a cover-up for a secret meeting to pass on that package whatever it was. It looks suspicious, and we're at war with Germany." She pulled the blanket closer. "Winnie will have to be told, but not a word to anyone else till we find out what's going on. Agreed?" The others nodded.

Lying under the doubled blankets next to Pearl, Jeanmarie thought about tall, stern Dr. Werner. "I remember the day Werner came to take me to the orphanage," she whispered. "The court worker with him said it would only be for a while to stay on a farm."

"M-m-m," Pearl said sleepily.

Jeanmarie sighed. A year had come and gone before she'd understood that she wasn't going home from Apple Valley Orphanage, not for a long time. Some kids, like her, were wards of the court because their parents couldn't keep them. They couldn't be adopted. But she'd never seen anyone else at the orphanage adopted either. Maybe it was the war. Of course once you were eighteen you had to leave the orphanage.

The sheet felt cold on her toes and she wiggled them. "Do you think Dr. Werner could really be working for the enemy?" she asked.

"People aren't always what they seem to be," Pearl murmured.

In the dark Jeanmarie lay still listening to Pearl's quiet breathing. If Dr. Werner was up to something they had to find out. She willed herself to be up as soon as the alarm went off in the morning. Pearl's bed would have to be put back in place before Mrs. Foster made her morning rounds. Jeanmarie knew she'd forgotten something, but she couldn't remember what, and her eyes were closing.

TWO

The Note

*P*earl was already up when Jeanmarie came awake and remembered what she'd forgotten the night before. It was Winnie's turn for kitchen duty. She'd promised to help her carry the heavy coal bucket from the cellar to the kitchen.

By the time Mrs. Foster passed the doorway in her robe and slippers, the beds were all neatly back in place, and Jeanmarie was dressed. Before anyone else came downstairs she and Winnie finished hauling the full coal bucket to the kitchen. "Go or you'll be late for your own work," Winnie urged.

"I'm off," Jeanmarie said, pulling her woolen scarf close to her chin. Cold air rushed to meet her as she left for her work at the farmhouse where some of the orphanage staff boarded. It was still dark as she pushed through the snow on the unplowed road. She was already late, and at every step her boots sank nearly to their tops slowing her walk.

Yellow light glowed in the windows of the farmhouse. Jeanmarie pushed open the cellar door and hurried to put her things on the coat peg. Inside her boots her feet sloshed in wet snow, but there was no time to take off her damp socks. Leaving her boots by her jacket she crammed on her dry shoes and slipped upstairs into the kitchen.

Gracie, a tall, pale girl with thin blonde braids wrapped round her head, was already arranging a tray of toast and jam to take to the staff dining room. As she passed Jeanmarie she whispered, "You're late."

"Sorry," Jeanmarie murmured. Of the four girls' cottages at the orphanage, Gracie's was closest to the farmhouse. She was always at work before Jeanmarie arrived.

Mrs. Koppel, the cook and housekeeper, stood with her back to Jeanmarie in front of the large, black iron coal stove. She was a short, stout woman who wore her hair on top of her head in a twisted bun that looked like a small knob. Her strong hands flew from the rigorous stirring of a pot of cereal to flipping eggs in the frying pan. Pausing long enough to look back, her black eyes glared at Jeanmarie. "So, late again, is it? And vat excuses now?"

Jeanmarie started to tell her about the deep snow, but Mrs. Koppel was in no mood to reason. "Never mind, go. Go make the beds. And ven you dust you shake the dust mop, do you hear?" She turned toward the stove with a groan. "Such goings-on. Never in my days vas I late." Jeanmarie hesitated, wondering if she should ask about her breakfast.

"Vell? Vat do you stand there for staring? You are too late for breakfast. So you vill learn to be on time. Go on, go on."

Jeanmarie's stomach rumbled as she walked the polished hall floor to the carpeted stair leading to the staff bedrooms.

Of all the jobs in the orphanage, why had she landed this one? Everybody else got to eat breakfast in their own cottages. Only she and Gracie had to trudge to the farmhouse, help Mrs. Koppel serve breakfast to the orphanage staff, make the beds, and tidy the staff rooms all before the school bell rang. Her stomach growled again urging her to hurry. She would have to eat half her lunch sandwich before school.

The first room on the left belonged to Mrs. Gillpin, who taught seventh and eighth grade. Mrs. Gillpin made her own bed and generally kept the room neat. A quick look around showed Jeanmarie there was little to do. As she turned to go, a stack of familiar school notebooks on the wide mahogany desk caught her eye. She straightened the notebooks and glanced at a paper lying next to them. An official war office stamp stood out across the top. Under it she saw the words *My Dearest*. Mrs. Gillpin must have forgotten to put away the letter from her Navy husband. Jeanmarie carefully put the letter back the way it had been.

Above the desk hung a map of the world like the one in school. Small paper flags pinned to it showed the battle sites. The black swastikas were for the enemy, the Axis: Germany, Japan, and Italy. The red, white, and blue flags stood for the Allies: the United States, England, and the others.

Next to the map hung a gold-framed picture of Mrs. Gillpin and her husband. The man in the photo was tall, dark-haired, and handsome in his Navy uniform. He could be anywhere in the world now on some ship. With her free hand Jeanmarie saluted the picture. "Good luck wherever you are, sir."

The farmer's room was different. Frowning, Jeanmarie picked up the bed pillow. Pressed deeply into the sheet were the marks of a set of false teeth. "Ugh," she said, flattening the pillow down hard where the teeth must have lain all night.

When the bed was finished she ran the dust mop around the edges of the rug. For good measure, she blew the dust off the nightstand. A pair of faded coveralls had slipped to the floor, and she hung them across the back of the stuffed armchair. The desk was clear except for an old ink pot, some toothpicks, and a few farm magazines addressed to George Banks, nothing exciting.

The last room down the hall belonged to the school bus driver, Sam. A short, thin, balding man with a limp, he loved to tease his riders. He had a sharp tongue, but Jeanmarie liked him. Souvenirs, trophies, and even a stuffed fish mounted on a wooden board spilled over the shelves and dresser top. It was a happy mess, and she was careful not to disturb it. Finished, she shook the dust mop out the window. Light snow was falling again.

The snow was still coming down when she and Gracie hurried off to school.

Gracie was indignant. "That Banks is one dumb farmer," she said as they trudged through the snow. "He's been here long enough to know a bowl of jam from his dish of fruit. He ate every bit of jam right out of the serving bowl!"

Jeanmarie shrugged between bites of her potted meat sandwich. "Maybe with false teeth he can't tell the difference between a dish of fruit and jam." Gracie snorted.

The smell of wet wool coats and rubber boots hovered in the school coatroom as Jeanmarie hung her things on a hook. "At least there's no chapel this morning," she said.

Gracie kicked off a boot. "Thank goodness. Another talk from Chaplain Stone and I'll turn into a stone."

Jeanmarie laughed. "You won't miss anything if you do. They all sound alike." The new chaplain at the orphanage seemed to like talking about following good examples. She'd heard better sermons back in the city in a storefront mission on 116th Street in Harlem. A sock came off in her boot and she fished it out.

At eight years old she had been the only white girl sitting with the children and their mothers listening to the missionary, Mother Anderson. There were never any fathers that she could see. She'd learned all about sin and hell and judgment from Mother Anderson's sermons. Chaplain Stone didn't come close to Mother Anderson. The late bell pierced her thoughts. Hastily, she shoved her half-eaten lunch onto the rack overhead.

Jeanmarie's classroom was the first of the orphanage's four classrooms for kindergarten through eighth grade. She was just in time to slip into the seventh and eighth grade room before the door closed. She slid into her seat and searched inside her desk for her notebook. Mrs. Gillpin rapped for attention. Jeanmarie glanced up, then stared at her teacher.

Looking like a half-made-up clown, Mrs. Gillpin had large black streaks under both eyes where trails of mascara had run partway down her cheeks. In contrast to the dark patches, her small, turned-up nose looked red, like a person's might with a bad cold or hard crying. Muffled laughter rippled through the room.

Mrs. Gillpin tapped a ruler against her desk for silence. Jeanmarie felt a wild urge to get up out of her seat and do something, but what? As the room quieted Mrs. Gillpin began taking attendance.

Pearl, whose desk was in front of Jeanmarie's, reached behind her and dropped a note. Quickly, Jeanmarie cupped it in her left hand.

"Radio news bad this morning," the note said. "Ship sunk right off east coast. Mr. G. Navy, any connection? S." The S was for Skinny, a nickname Pearl hated but used on her notes. On the bottom half of the note Jeanmarie wrote, "Saw letter on G.'s desk—Navy address. G. looks terrible."

When Mrs. Gillpin moved from behind her desk several of the boys snickered, but Mrs. Gillpin didn't seem to hear them. "Robert, will you get the battle flags, please," she said.

Jeanmarie sighed. There was nothing anyone could do but pretend not to notice Mrs. Gillpin's face. One by one the flags were pinned to the large map, the tiny Axis flags off Malaya, Java, and India outnumbering the Allied flags. In Denmark, Yugoslavia, Greece, Norway, and deep into Russia the enemy Axis flags marched boldly.

"Now, class," Mrs. Gillpin said, "we must be thankful for the good news. The Russian troops are fighting splendidly against the Germans. And in Egypt Rommel has not advanced in four days." Clearing her throat she added softly, "And of course General MacArthur's brave troops are still defending northwest of Manila in spite of heavy Japanese bombing and some losses."

Wilfred, the class brain, oblivious to Mrs. Gillpin's clown-like appearance, raised his hand for attention. "Listen to this, Mrs. Gillpin," he said, pointing to the thick *New York Times* in front of him. "Ten German suspects seized in sabotage attempt in Suffolk and Nassau counties. Pictures of members of the German American Bund club used to help identify suspects." He pushed his round owl glasses back onto his nose and read: "This brings the number of aliens seized since Pearl Harbor to 2,211. Of these, 1,430 Germans have been arrested." Wilfred ran a hand through his thick, black hair. "Wow, Suffolk and Nassau are practically in our backyard."

"It isn't likely that we will find spies here in Apple Valley," Mrs. Gillpin said. "However, outside the orphanage grounds is another story. I don't think we need to worry, class, not with J. Edgar Hoover and the FBI at work for Uncle Sam."

Jeanmarie looked up from the list of suspects with German names she was writing inside her English notebook. Before last night she might have thought the same thing. But Apple Valley Orphanage might not be at all the safe place it looked. Much as she doubted it would lead anywhere, she added Mrs. Koppel's name under Dr. Werner's. Just for fairness, she put Hans, Mrs. K.'s handsome bachelor son, underneath his mother's name.

After lunch a quiet but clean-faced Mrs. Gillpin returned to class and began the afternoon reading sessions, keeping both classes busy working at a steady pace.

There was still one more chore Jeanmarie had to do at the farmhouse—empty the staff wastebaskets. If there was time before Mrs. Gillpin returned home from school, Jeanmarie would look around in her room for clues to what might have upset her. On the list of questions, under "S. WITH ACCENT?" Jeanmarie drew a heavy black line. Who could the stranger with Dr. Werner have been?

At 2:30 the unexpected happened. "Tess," Mrs. Gillpin said, "would you mind staying after school to help with some artwork? I'll give you a late pass for work."

Tess was the class artist. She glanced at Jeanmarie and shrugged. "Yes, ma'am," she said quietly.

Jeanmarie frowned. It meant Tess wouldn't have time to look for Luke to ask him about last night. From the back of the room someone sneezed, and she turned to look—Winnie. Win could do it. On her way to sewing Winnie passed the barn too. Quickly Jeanmarie scribbled a note, folded it, marked it "Winnie," and sent it behind her. Only it wasn't Winnie who grabbed it.

Emma, her dark blonde hair sweeping Jeanmarie's face as she passed, held the note high in her left fist.

"That's mine," Jeanmarie whispered fiercely. Emma smiled and continued on her way to the pencil sharpener.

Inwardly Jeanmarie groaned. Though they lived in the same cottage, Emma Jones had been her personal enemy from day one at the orphanage.

Emma came back down the aisle, and Jeanmarie looked at her fiercely. "Give it back!" she demanded in a low voice.

Emma tossed her head. "Not on your life," she whispered.

Jeanmarie felt her face growing scarlet and turned away. What could Emma do with it anyway? All the note said was, "Can you take Tess's place? Ask Luke about last night. Jm."

A low laugh made her look at the boys' row. Jerry Green held her note in his hand. Grinning, he passed it up the row. Ten minutes later the entire left side of the room had read it.

Helpless, Jeanmarie tried to ignore the whispers and coughs to get her attention. She hadn't expected Emma to be so clever. From now on she would be more careful.

By the sixth time someone whispered to her, "Don't worry; I'll be happy to ask Luke about last night," the forced smile on Jeanmarie's face felt unbearably tight. For once she was glad to escape to the farmhouse.

In the warm kitchen Hans Koppel sat visiting with his mother. Young and tall with curly, black hair, Hans was handsome. He smiled at Jeanmarie as she passed.

"Ja, Mutter, ja," he said, turning back to Mrs. Koppel. Jeanmarie stood still in the middle of the kitchen. That accent, it was as if she were hearing it for the first time. "Ja, Mutter."

Could Hans have been the one with Dr. Werner last night? But what about the car? Hans always rode the mail truck to visit his mother and walked back to town. Maybe he'd borrowed a car.

Mrs. Koppel was looking at her, waiting, and Jeanmarie hurried into the hallway. If Hans was running secret errands, what about Mrs. Koppel? Was she mixed up in it too? Deep inside she couldn't believe the housekeeper would betray her country even though the thought of Mrs. Koppel being questioned by the FBI was tempting. She sighed and quickened her pace.

In the kitchen Hans laughed loudly. Jeanmarie listened, raised an eyebrow, and went on. If Dr. Werner wasn't what he seemed to be, Hans Koppel might not be either.

THREE

A Close Call

*T*he cottage seemed dangerously quiet as Jeanmarie slid open her dresser drawer slowly, trying not to make a sound. Mrs. Foster was in her rooms with the door closed, and Jeanmarie could hear the low sound of a radio. The others had already gone down to the gym for the Saturday night movie. She and Pearl had stayed behind in the cellar waiting for everyone else to leave when she'd remembered the flashlight. They'd come back upstairs to find it.

"Hurry up!" Pearl whispered. "If Foster finds us here she'll never let us go. Never mind the flashlight."

"Got it," Jeanmarie said. She grabbed the flashlight from the corner of the drawer where it had rolled under a sweater and stuck it inside her jacket. The drawer squeaked as she shut it, and a stab of fear

27

rushed through her. If they were caught she didn't have an excuse for being here this late.

"Come on," Pearl begged. "If she catches us we could be on restrictions till New Year's." Restrictions meant no movies, no weekend privileges like passes for off-ground walks, no radio. Jeanmarie had lost count of the time she had spent on Mrs. Foster's restriction list.

"Right," she said softly. This was no time to panic.

Silently, she led the way downstairs, through the cellar, and out the back door.

Against the corner of the house Tess waited for them. She was almost invisible in the shadows. With her thick black hair stuffed into a wool cap she looked all business. "It's about time you two got here," she said. "Emma left with Leah and the others ten minutes ago."

"Good," Jeanmarie said. "Those two have been watching me all day just hoping for a clue to that note about Luke." Aside from the fact that Emma had chosen Jeanmarie as an enemy, she and Leah kept on the good side of Mrs. Foster by informing on others. Luckily, the two of them slept in the younger girls' dorm.

"If all goes well, the only thing we have to worry about is watching our time," she said. It was a big *if.* Like shadows, the three of them raced down the hill, past the light of the street lamps to the cluster of buildings below.

Breathing hard Jeanmarie stopped and leaned against the dark wall behind the gym. Somewhere inside, Winnie and Maria would be carrying out their parts of the plan. Tonight they were sitting in separate parts of the huge gym instead of together as they usually did. It would be difficult for anyone looking for the group to spot who was there and who wasn't. By now the lights were off, and the movie had begun.

Jeanmarie signaled to Tess, and one by one they slipped into the street and headed to the barn.

The barn smelled of cows and oldness, but at least it was warmer than outside, and it was safe. No one would be coming by on a Saturday night. Jeanmarie lit her flashlight to look at the scrap of paper clutched tightly in her left hand. Maria had found it in a trash basket while cleaning the Werners' study.

Aloud she read, "Contact through K. Arrange delivery. Replace B. That could be B for Luke Boyd," she said. The list went on. "Take money and marker, pick up freezer key on way, delivery Thursday." She looked up. "That could mean Thursday, the night of the air-raid practice."

Pearl nodded. "And doesn't he always go into the city on Thursdays? It could mean he delivers something to the city."

In the silence mixed with the restless movements of the cows in the stalls Jeanmarie stared at the paper in her hand. The words "pick up freezer key" must mean the key to the huge cold storage building where the orphanage meat supply was kept. It was the only freezer she knew about. Farmer Banks kept the key somewhere here in the barn, but where?

"This whole thing is crazy," Tess said. "It's like trying to picture Dr. Werner in a zoot suit holding up a bank."

Pearl pushed her cap back from her forehead. "I read about a spy in the Revolutionary War who owned a pewter store and passed on messages to the enemy on his weekly trips to town," she said glumly.

Jeanmarie nodded. "We'd better get on with it if we're going to find that key." She turned toward an empty cow stall. "That's Banks's office over there. Last fall I brought his supper down here on the day they butchered pigs. There were two or three keys on his desk when I put the tray on it." She'd left in a hurry, hating the sounds of the squealing pigs in the barnyard.

The farmer's office was little more than a boxlike room with a chair and a desk covered with papers and old notebooks. They'd gone over everything twice by the time Pearl warned them that in thirty or so minutes they had to be back at the gym or the movie would let out without them.

Jeanmarie sighed. Banks might have taken the keys back to the farmhouse with him. Once more she checked the pockets of the coveralls hanging on a nail next to a large calendar. Slowly she searched the dark wood walls looking for pegs or nails that might hold the key they needed. Nothing; she was back to where the calendar hung. For a moment she stared at the string holding the calendar. Behind it hanging straight down from the nail was a key. On the back of the key handle a small tag read "locker."

Jeanmarie held it up in triumph. "This is it! We can open the freezer, find the package, put the key back, and be at the gym on time." Without waiting for comments she was on the way to the cold storage, a square cement building about fifty feet from the barn.

Tess held the heavy door while they slipped inside. The room was cavelike. Giant chunks of meat, some with a leg still attached, hung from metal hooks on the walls. It was cold too, a deep, chilling cold. Shivering, Jeanmarie swung her light slowly about, glad that most of the hooks were empty.

Ahead of her Pearl beamed her light into the inner room. "We've had it," she called, shaking her head.

"What's that supposed to mean?" Tess asked, crowding in next to her.

"See for yourself," Pearl answered, stepping aside. On every wall were shelves with boxes. All of them were sealed with tape and marked in heavy black marker. All of them looked the same except for the code on each—a number and the word *chic* or *sa*. "We don't know what we're supposed to look for," she said. "We can't open them all, and besides, we're running out of time."

If only one package were different somehow, Jeanmarie thought, but maybe this wasn't even the freezer the note referred to after all. She turned to follow Pearl and Tess, felt for the key in her jacket pocket, and sighed. They had run into the unexpected. Though what she had expected she didn't know.

"Hey, the door won't open!" Pearl cried. "There isn't any lock on this side, and I can't budge the handle!" Jeanmarie held Pearl's flashlight while Tess added her weight to Pearl's to push against the door. Then Tess held the light while Jeanmarie tried. The door, solid metal with a large handle, wouldn't budge. The handle turned no more than a fraction of an inch.

Cold sweat ran down Jeanmarie's back under her woolen jacket as she put her shoulder to the handle and tried to force it. "It's stuck, really stuck. I can't get it to move!" she panted. Tess's face was white in the light of the flashlight that shook in her hands. At her feet Pearl slumped in a heap on the floor, a bundle of despair. "Think of something, Pearl," Jeanmarie cried.

"I am thinking!" Pearl shouted. "We're going to die in here, that's what I'm thinking, and the only thing we can do is try to get help." She began banging against the door with her feet, and shouting, "Help, somebody help get us out of here!" Soon the three of them were shouting and banging on the door.

"Stop, stop, shush a minute," Pearl commanded. Jeanmarie stood motionless; beside her Tess held her breath.

From outside the door came a muffled voice. "Who are you, and what're you doing in there anyway?"

"It's me, Pearl, and Jeanmarie and Tess. Please get us out of here; the door won't open!" They listened as the person on the other side pushed against the door.

"I can't; it's locked," the voice said. "I need the key to open it."

"I have the key!" Jeanmarie shouted. "I've got the key in here, but there isn't any lock on this side."

"I know," said the voice, "the lock is outside, and when you open it, you're supposed to fix the lock so it stays open until you leave. Obviously, you dimwits didn't know that."

Jeanmarie was already kneeling close to the bottom of the door, feeling the rubber flap that ran along its edge to help insulate the locker. "Listen, I think I can push the key under the door, okay?"

"Okay," the voice on the other side answered. Jeanmarie shoved the key as far under the strip as she could and waited, not daring to breathe. When the door opened she practically fell into a surprised Luke's arms.

"Listen, you guys, I don't know what you've been up to, but stealing isn't my cup of tea. What were you doing in there?" His voice was stern, his blue eyes boring into them.

Too glad to be indignant, Jeanmarie quickly explained. "We weren't stealing or anything like that. It was all a big mistake, and we have to get back to the gym now or somebody will notice we're not there." Pearl was frantically pointing to her watch.

"Yeah, get out of here before I get into trouble," Luke said gruffly. "Only the next time I see you, you'd better have a good story. And leave me out of this, hear? If I hadn't been coming home from off-grounds work, you could have been in there all night." He shook his head. "I don't mind doing a favor, but keep it quiet. I don't need any trouble. Mum's the word, got it?"

Solemnly, Jeanmarie promised that he could count on them.

"One thing," she said. "Did Dr. Werner take air-raid duty for you on Thursday night?"

Luke looked puzzled. "He let us all off. It was snowing. Anyway, what's that got to do with all this?"

Pearl was already running toward the gym, Tess close behind her. Jeanmarie smiled and ran after them. At least she'd found out something. She slipped her hand into her jacket pocket and felt for the key. Her pocket was empty. Luke had the key!

It was too late now to go back. Any minute kids would be coming out of the gym, and they had to be there to mix with the crowd. Luke was probably gone by now. Had he remembered the key? Would he put it back in the barn? Did he know where Mr. Banks kept it? All the older boys helped with the farming, but what if Luke didn't know where to hang the key? Her stomach felt as if she'd eaten too many green apples.

She reached Pearl and Tess in the shadows by the side of the gym as the doors opened, letting out a bedlam of voices into the night, and whispered, "The key, Luke has the key." The meaning dawned on Pearl's face, and she moaned. Tess frowned.

Others passed them, laughing and jostling, taking no notice of the three who joined them. Jeanmarie could think of nothing to say as they walked in silence.

Unfortunately they had chosen to mix with Emma's group. Even in pale moonlight Emma's look seemed suspicious. "So, how'd you like the movie?" Emma asked, poking her cohort Leah's thin arm. She was speaking directly to Jeanmarie.

Jeanmarie's senses came wide awake. "Oh, it was okay, if you know what I mean," she muttered, continuing to walk steadily up the hill.

Emma was not to be so easily put off. Pushing her way closer to Jeanmarie she said loudly, "Who do you think should have won her?"

Jeanmarie felt panic rising in her throat. Emma wanted an argument. She had no idea what the movie had been. How could she even guess? Did Emma know that she hadn't been there at all? Was she just playing a game with them like a cat with a mouse ready to pounce any minute? Jeanmarie dreaded the words she thought were coming—"You weren't at the movies, and I'm going to report you to Mrs. Foster."

Only the voice that spoke up wasn't Emma's; it was Maria's. "Well, actually, there was never any real question of Glenn Miller not getting Tess Hutton. 'Moonlight Serenade' was made for them, don't you think?" She went on and on, never giving Emma a chance to say anything.

Maria had saved them this time. But what about the key to the locker? If Luke went home with the key and Banks found out it was gone, what then? Would Luke turn them in along with the key?

FOUR

The Key

The iron steeple bell above the orphanage building that housed the school and chapel was still clanging as the girls' choir hurriedly dressed for church. Jeanmarie wriggled her head into the white, starched surplice, pulling it down over her black choir gown; the full sleeves stuck out on either side like angels' wings. Pressing down the ballooning sides of her surplice she took her place in line. The march into the narrow choir stalls at the front of the chapel was the part she always dreaded. On this Sunday nothing unusual happened, and Jeanmarie slid into her seat, thankful that she hadn't tripped over her own feet.

Twice she almost caught Luke's eye during the service, but there was little she could do besides stare. Where was the key to the freezer? Had Luke put it back? In front of her, every face in chapel seemed to be looking directly at her. Farmer Banks's face was not among them. Maybe he hadn't discovered that the key was missing yet. That would give them time today to put it back if no one was around, if Luke hadn't left it in the door; if, if, if. She squirmed in the crowded stall and accidentally kicked Tess's foot. "Sorry," she mouthed.

By the time church was over and they'd changed out of their robes, Luke was gone. "I couldn't catch Luke," Winnie said as she joined Jeanmarie and the others. "But I heard him tell Irene he would see her later today during visiting hours." On alternate Sunday afternoons any of the older boys could be invited for a visit at the girls' cottages. Irene was one of the older girls in Wheelock.

"We'll have to catch him before he reaches the cottage," Jeanmarie said. There was no way they could get to him under the watchful eye of Mrs. Foster. During visiting hours while the girls talked with their guests in Wheelock's living room, Mrs. Foster would sit in her rocking chair, knitting and watching until the last boy left.

The three hours before visiting time loomed like forever. Jeanmarie didn't even know if Luke had the key, and worse, she still had to explain what they'd been doing in the freezer Saturday night.

In spite of her worries it was a perfect winter day, clear and sunny. At the edge of the yard the youngest orphans in Wheelock were building a large snowman. The tallest, her red hair poking out from under her cap and falling across her small freckled face, waved; Jeanmarie waved back. As she did she noticed a car driving up the road toward the cottage. Rarely did any car other than Dr. Werner's enter the grounds. The limousine, shiny, black, and longer than two normal cars, pulled up in front of Wheelock. A chauffeur, smartly outfitted in a green uniform, held open the door for an older man in a fur-trimmed overcoat. The second passenger, a woman smothered in shining furs, stepped out behind him. The two led the way toward the cottage followed by the chauffeur carrying several large boxes. At once the smaller girls left to fall in line behind them.

"It's her," Maria whispered. For the last two years the same woman had brought Christmas candy in similar boxes.

"She always looks sad," Pearl said. "Maybe she lost her own child and wants to adopt one of us, but her husband won't let her, so she brings candy each Christmas hoping he might change his mind when he sees us."

"And do you suppose it's you they might be looking for and don't know it?" Jeanmarie asked jokingly.

"Who knows?" Pearl said. "I can dream, can't I? And maybe somebody in this orphanage really is a lost heiress."

Jeanmarie sat back on her heels in the snow and glanced at the waiting limo. Strange things could happen. Of the five of them she was the only one who knew who her parents were. The little girls had come outside again and stood in a small group waiting for the visitors. All four were orphans with no families. "Well there's four little ones," Jeanmarie said, "just waiting for a real mother."

The woman had come out followed by the gentleman and the chauffeur. Jeanmarie watched her walk to the car, smiling and waving good-bye.

Pearl sighed as the limo pulled away. "Anyway, there goes our limo till next year." She plopped down on the snow beside Jeanmarie along with the others.

"Okay," Jeanmarie said. "We still have a war going on, and there's work to do." She began tracing lines in a sort of pattern on the flattened snow before her.

"What's that?" Pearl asked.

"Oh, just a map of the buildings around the barn," Jeanmarie answered in a casual voice.

"Oh no," Maria moaned, "you're not going to try and find that package again?"

Tess's brown eyes were wide in her square face as she looked first at the map, then at Jeanmarie. "Are you out of your mind? One time was enough. If we try the freezer again, we're pushing our luck. Besides, we all agreed it was hopeless."

Jeanmarie pointed to the barn. "Who's going back to the freezer? What we have to figure out is how to get that key back on its hook if Luke hasn't already put it there." She looked up. "If Luke has the key, I say now is the time to act. We could be down there in five minutes, have one of us slip in the barn, and presto—the key is safely back." She hoped she looked more hopeful than her insides felt, but they had to put that key back.

As if on cue, Luke, dressed in his Sunday suit, came striding up the hill. He slowed as he neared them. "Listen, you sprats, I don't want to catch you again in lockers or barns or anywhere else you don't belong." His clear blue eyes searched their faces. "I don't know what you were up to, and I don't have time to hear it now. Just stay out of trouble." Not waiting for an answer he continued walking, then turned to say: "The key is back where it belongs. I gotta go."

For a moment his words hung in the air, then registered. The girls were safe. Jeanmarie could hardly believe it. "It's back; you mean it's back in the barn," she said. "Thanks, Luke. You really saved us from a pile of trouble."

"Yeah, well, I still want the whole story but not now. Got a date." Luke glanced at his watch and strode off up the hill toward Wheelock Cottage.

Once more he called back over his shoulder. "Banks will find it okay. I left it on the floor near his desk so he'll think it fell off without him noticing. Smart, eh?"

Jeanmarie winced. Banks might be at least fifty years old, and true, he couldn't tell the jam dish from dessert; still it was risky. Would he really think he had been careless with the key? "I guess one of us could go back and hang it up," she said softly.

One look at Pearl's face—thin lips pressed firmly closed, a solid, unyielding look in her eyes—made Jeanmarie shrug her shoulders. "Well, if you are all against it, that's that." With a kick she wiped out the map. "Maria, you're still our best bet to find out what you can at the Werners' house. If Werner's working for the enemy by passing on packages of some kind, we have to find out what's going on and soon."

"Whoa," Tess said. "We can't do anything until Monday anyway, right? And that hill looks great for racing. No one is using those old sleds in the cellar." Tess looked longingly down the steep road. "Anybody want to go?"

Jeanmarie hesitated. With the key back in its place, or almost in place, everything should be okay until tomorrow. Why waste the afternoon? "I'm in," she said. Even though they didn't have permission to sled downhill on the road, Mrs. Foster never bothered to check outdoors, especially on a Sunday. Under her breath Jeanmarie whistled an old Irish tune from somewhere in her past as they went for the sleds.

The packed snow on the road was perfect, and she lost track of time. Hours later, standing at the top of the hill watching the others, she began to feel the cold creeping inside her jacket. The streetlight near her flickered on; the snow that had begun to fall whirled in its yellow light.

She heard someone in the distance call, "Good night!" Visiting hours must have ended; it was Luke still lingering by Wheelock's front porch. He came running to make up for lost time. "Hi, sprat," he called as he drew near. "Listen, don't you forget, mum's the word about that key."

"Right," she said, waving him on. Turning to pick up her sled she froze. Not three feet away, pulling a sled behind her, was Leah. Without saying a word the girl passed her and headed for the cottage. Jeanmarie groaned. Leah must have heard Luke mention the key. Leah would tell Emma, and nothing would stop the two of them from trying to find out more. It could only mean trouble.

FIVE

Stolen Chickens

With Monday morning's pile of fresh towels for the farmhouse staff under one arm and the day's newspapers under the other, Jeanmarie hurried up the stairs and down the hallway. She nearly collided with Farmer Banks, who was coming out of Mrs. Gillpin's room. Puzzled, Jeanmarie looked at him. Mrs. Gillpin always returned from her weekends away just in time for school and never went to her room until after school.

Mr. Banks looked embarrassed. Rubbing nervously at his long, drooping mustache, he murmured, "Wrong room, wrong turn." His shoulders stooped slightly as he shook his gray head. Jeanmarie nodded at him. It was a wonder how he managed to run the farm.

On the other hand, he might be getting old, but he was still strong.

The orphanage supplied all its own meat, milk, and vegetables. It was Banks himself who did the butchering. That took strength. The older boys helped, but most of the killing and cutting up was done by Banks. Jeanmarie shuddered. She hated the killing times. Hated afterwards when the pigs' heads with their staring glassy eyes arrived at each cottage to be made into headcheese, a thing she would never eat. The thought of it turned her stomach. She slipped into the teacher's room.

Mrs. Gillpin's bed was neat as usual. Jeanmarie left the towels in the bathroom, then stopped to check the desk. A tiny paper cutout ship with *S. S. McClellan* written on it lay on its side. She picked it up to look at it more closely. On the map above the desk an empty straight pin stuck out just off the east coast of the United States.

Curious, Jeanmarie held the paper ship next to it a moment before she put it back on the desk. As she did she noticed an official-looking envelope bearing the war office stamp. Gently she picked it up. Had Mr. Gillpin written to his wife and told her the name of his ship? Was that why the paper cutout *S. S. McClellan* lay on the desk and the empty pin waited on the map?

"Not off to school yet, eh?" The voice of Hans Koppel fell on Jeanmarie's ears like a net. She dropped the letter onto the desk and stared at him, her face burning. Hans set the toolbox he was carrying down by the radiator. "So our little teacher says this old thing is too noisy, ja. I will let out the air, and so we fix it," he said and smiled at her.

She had forgotten that Hans often did odd jobs for his mother on his day off. "I was just leaving," she said. Her face still burned. Had Hans seen her with Mrs. Gillpin's letter? She left without looking back.

Knocking hard on Mr. Banks's door, she held out his towels. He took them without a word, shutting the door immediately. "Rude," she whispered to the closed door. On the other hand, she thought, he might not have his teeth in.

Sam's room was next. She was confident that he would not be there since the high school kids had left on the bus into town half an hour ago. Sam's bedclothes lay in a tangled heap that took her several minutes to undo and straighten. When the bed was once more presentable, its striped spread met the pillow stripes exactly. Meanwhile the school bell had begun to clang a warning to the laggards to hurry. Jeanmarie raced.

By the time she reached the school everyone else had gone in except for two small figures coming slowly down the steps. It was May with a glum-looking Kathy behind her. "Whoa," Jeanmarie said, reaching out for May's arm. "Aren't you two going in the wrong direction?"

May hung her head trying to avoid Jeanmarie's eyes, but Kathy's answer was quick and to the point. "Mrs. Dingle sent May home, and I'm supposed to see that she gets there."

Jeanmarie lifted the small girl's chin to look at her. "Why is your teacher sending you home, May, are you sick?" The child just shook her head.

"She's not sick; she's wet," Kathy explained.

Jeanmarie was shocked. "Wet, like wet pants? Is that it?" May nodded miserably. "But you never have accidents like that. How did it happen?"

"Emma," Kathy said. "She took May's pencil and eraser because she forgot her own and the gingerbread from her lunchbag too." Kathy put a protective arm around May's shoulder. "And then she squeezed her hand real hard, and said that if she told anybody she'd squeeze it even harder or something lots worse."

"That's when I got wet," May said quietly.

Jeanmarie took May's hands gently in her own mittened ones. "Never mind," she said. "Don't you worry about Emma anymore. I'll see to it as soon as I can. Go on home and get changed so you don't miss too much." She watched the two children head toward the hill. "And don't forget to pick up a pencil and eraser for yourself," she called. That Emma. Somebody had to stop her.

The moment Jeanmarie dreaded came as she faced Emma in the cottage kitchen. Emma's face grew dark, her fists clenched. No one else was in the kitchen. Jeanmarie stood her ground. "You can't scare little kids and get away with it," she heard herself say.

Emma smiled a slow, deliberate smile. "And what makes you so concerned anyway," she said. "They're making it all up, you know. You can't prove a thing, and besides, I didn't do it. You can ask Leah. I was with her the whole time."

Jeanmarie took a deep breath. "May doesn't lie. If she says you bullied her, then you did."

Emma exploded. "You think you can pick on me. That May is a little liar! You had better watch who you're accusing." Menace in her voice and in her eyes, she advanced toward Jeanmarie. Like a sudden storm erupting she pushed Jeanmarie hard against the kitchen wall.

Jeanmarie felt rather than saw Emma's hands around her throat, her thick, smothering hair in her face. Instinctively, her fingers twisted in Emma's long hair, pulling hard.

"Help, Mrs. Foster, help!" Emma screamed. Jeanmarie held on against Emma's wild, flailing fists. Suddenly she felt strong fingers digging into her shoulders, gripping and pulling her away from Emma.

Mrs. Foster glared at them both. "What's going on here?" she thundered. Grasping Jeanmarie's wrist she forced open the fingers still clutching Emma's long, straw-blonde hairs. "Why, you little scamp. Hand me one of those envelopes on the shelf," she directed. Emma handed her an envelope.

44

Still holding tight to Jeanmarie's arm she shook the hair, a startling amount, into the envelope. She handed the sealed envelope to Jeanmarie. "You march yourself down to Dr. Werner's office and give him this envelope with poor Emma's hair in it, while I call him and tell him about this. Let him decide what to do with you." Turning to Emma she said, "Now you go along too and get this straightened out." She pointed to the door. "And mind, I don't want to hear of a word passed between you on the way down. You hear?"

Jeanmarie trembled. Without speaking she flung her jacket on and left. It wasn't fair. Mrs. Foster didn't want to know what had happened. A scratch on Jeanmarie's chin smarted, and she rubbed it. She felt like running, running till she reached home, her own home wherever it was now. She hadn't meant to pull Emma's hair, and she would probably get it from Dr. Werner.

Would he paddle her? She had never been disciplined by him before, but she had seen the angry red marks on the face of a boy who had. Most of the housemothers used apple switches. She almost wished Mrs. Foster did. It would have been better than facing Dr. Werner. Her stomach was beginning to feel slightly sick. Emma followed close on her heels, and Jeanmarie quickened her step without looking back.

The hallway to Dr. Werner's office was deserted except for their echoing footsteps on the stone floor. The door was closed, but from behind it came the loud, demanding voice of Dr. Werner.

"Are you telling me that someone, somehow, got into the freezer and stole a dozen boxes of chicken? How is it possible? There are no windows, the door is metal, and the lock sturdy. How could it happen?"

"I'm trying to tell you, sir. Someone stole the key, let themselves in, and returned the key to my office." Jeanmarie recognized Farmer Banks's voice. "I found the key on the floor next to the desk. Whoever it was must have been scared off and left in a hurry, too quickly to put the key back in its place. They just tossed it."

"That key is a sacred trust." Dr. Werner's voice was outraged. "You, sir, should have seen to it. From now on you are to lock it properly inside your desk."

Jeanmarie gulped. Dr. Werner didn't mention that he had taken the freezer key, at least he'd written "pick up freezer key" on the list Maria had found. And who had taken the chickens? Surely not Luke!

"Leave the key with me," Dr. Werner ordered. "I suppose I'll have to go check for myself. This is the last kind of publicity we need. I've half a mind not to report it at all."

"Well, sir, I was thinking that we could keep a tight watch ourselves. Whoever it was won't get away with it a second time."

"Yes, Banks, a good idea. I'll put a few of the boys on watch tonight. Tomorrow we'll have a lock and a proper door on your office. And, Banks, not a word of this in town. Do you understand? Bad publicity, and the next thing you know we'll have a lot of nosey reporters out here."

When the door opened Jeanmarie and Emma stood aside as Banks rushed past without seeming to notice them.

Dr. Werner stared at the two of them, a puzzled look on his face. "Well? What is it? Speak up."

With a look of wounded innocence Emma went inside and stood before him. Absently, he reached for the envelope Jeanmarie held out. "Yes, oh that. Mrs. Foster called me. Sit," he commanded, waving the envelope toward the two chairs in front of his desk.

Jeanmarie sat stiffly, facing the enormous mahogany desk and braced herself for what she knew was coming.

"Such nonsense. You know that young ladies do not settle their differences by pulling out one another's hair. You would both be bald in no time. If I am not mistaken, it seems to me that you are calm enough now." Dr. Werner rapped his knuckles against the top of his desk. Each time his hands moved, Jeanmarie expected they would reach for the wooden paddle hanging on the wall behind him. Though her knees were knocking, she kept her head high. Next to her Emma sniffled.

As they waited in the overheated office for Dr. Werner to go on, Jeanmarie wanted desperately to take off her jacket, but she didn't dare draw attention to herself.

Dr. Werner might have been miles away from the look on his face when he suddenly glanced at them as if seeing them for the first time. "So let this visit be a warning to you. I want you to return to your cottage and behave yourselves. Another time I shall not hesitate to punish you. It is the season of our Savior's birth. Let us have peace, young ladies, peace. Now go."

Jeanmarie could hardly believe her ears—no restrictions, no paddling, no scolding. Stammering thanks, she slid from the chair, stumbling a little in her haste to reach the door. Behind her Emma too wasted no time in her rush to leave the administration building and its forbidding cold stone corridors.

"Now what's that all about?" Emma muttered half to herself. "He must be mighty worried about those chicken thieves." She turned to look directly at Jeanmarie. "Just don't think I'll forget."

Before Jeanmarie could answer, two of Emma's friends from James Cottage hailed her. Emma stopped to talk, and Jeanmarie continued walking past. With a sigh she let out a puff of white breath that hung for an instant in the winter

47

air. All the while Emma had been near she could think of nothing but the key. The last thing she wanted Emma to remember was Luke telling her "to keep mum about the key." Maybe Leah hadn't reported their conversation.

The missing chickens was a new piece of information. It didn't make sense to her. If Werner had taken the key, wasn't it to put a package into the freezer? Or did he take something out—the chickens maybe? Banks had found the key on the floor by the desk, but Luke had put it there. So when did the theft really happen? Maybe the thief found the key on the floor, stole the chickens, then put the key back on the floor. One thought startled her. Could Luke have decided to take the chickens? But why? She couldn't believe it of Luke. She hurried on. Outside the orphanage that chicken was worth a whole lot on the black market. Meat was scarce because of the war. She walked quickly.

Pearl was waiting for her, worry in her eyes. "How did it go?"

"Strangest thing you ever heard," Jeanmarie replied. "This time he let us off. Said it was Christmas and a time for peace." She hadn't thought of it before, but Christmas was almost here. "But have I got news. Where is everybody?"

Pearl nodded her head in the direction of the living room. "Wait; before you go in," she said, "there's a letter for you. It came in this afternoon's mail. I laid it on your bed."

"Thanks. I'll read it and be right down with the news." Letters from anyone were rare enough to make them special events. Seated on her cot Jeanmarie opened the envelope carefully. The handwriting was her mother's.

Dear Jeanmarie,

I trust you are well and being a good girl. I would have liked to come and see you, but you know how it is. Your dad and me don't get along and it's best

*we don't meet. We had a little run-in last week.
Nothing serious, and I had a day's leave coming to
me anyway. Too bad the army won't take him on
account of his flat feet.*

Jeanmarie stopped reading and stared out the window.
Why did things like that have to happen? She hardly ever saw
her mother, because she could never come on a visiting Sunday in case her father did. And he came, wanted or not. Jeanmarie read the rest of the letter. It was mostly about the factory her mother worked at, helping with the war effort.
Finished, she folded it carefully and put it inside her keep-
sake box with the others. Hastily she looked around then
quickly bowed her head.

"Dear God, it's me, Jeanmarie. Please keep my mom from
having run-ins with my dad. And please help us win the war.
I'll try to be good. Thanks." Something wet slid down her
cheek, and she wiped it away with the back of her hand. It
had been a hard day.

SIX

Suspicion

Jeanmarie stepped over a dust mop lying on the hall floor. It was already morning chore time, and Lizzie and Rosie were sweeping the far end of the hall. The broom handle was twice as tall as either of them.

"Bye!" they called. Jeanmarie blew them a kiss. At the foot of the stairs she passed the dining room and glanced inside. Emma and Leah, deep in conversation, were setting tables. Both girls looked up in time to catch her eye. Had they been discussing her? There was no time to think about it now. Hurrying by, she opened and shut the cellar door behind her with a bang.

The warmth of the furnace and the faint, familiar smell of coal gas enveloped her. She took her jacket from its peg and stuck her arms into the sleeves. In winter the odor from the coal burnt in the furnace and upstairs stove permeated everything in the house. She was used to it, and her jacket, warmed by the furnace, felt good.

Outside, gray clouds covered the sky like a great, sagging cloth. No sun could possibly make its way through. Was it an omen of the day to come?

When Jeanmarie reached the farmhouse, things were in an uproar. Mrs. Koppel was waving her spatula in the air like a red flag. Mrs. Gillpin was out of town for a week, which meant one less to serve, but Gracie was home sick with a sore throat, and that meant one less to help with the work.

"The poor voman has other things in life besides you school children," Mrs. Koppel said, emphasizing her words with her swinging spatula. Jeanmarie knew she meant Mrs. Gillpin. "Who should know better than me, these things," Mrs. Koppel continued.

"You," she ordered, pointing Jeanmarie toward the kitchen table, "eat. Vun I got sick today, and this vun stands here dreaming."

Biting her tongue, Jeanmarie hurriedly sat down to eat her breakfast—hot cereal again. Without Gracie she would have to do double duty, but at least she could eat first. For the next hour Jeanmarie had no time to think. When the school bell rang she flew out the door, glad to escape.

Confusion reigned in grades seven and eight. Pearl turned around as Jeanmarie took her seat. "The new sub's Miss Dove, and the way she looks she'll need all the help she can get," Pearl said softly.

There was no need for notes this morning. Jeanmarie looked at the slender young woman standing in front of the classroom, smiling bravely. She was willow thin. Long, straight, blonde hair hung midway down her back. No one would take her seriously. Jeanmarie was glad for her sake

JEANMARIE and the FBI

that at least it wasn't spring. In winter you could assume no
toads or snakes, but even so she glanced over at the boys'
desks, wondering what tricks they would think up.

Miss Dove made the first mistake of the day during social
studies. "Now, classes, while you work on your workbook
assignments I want you to feel free to come up and use the
reference books. You may talk to a fellow student about the
subject if you like, and just make this an enjoyable learn-
ing time." She smiled sweetly and sat down at her desk
expectantly.

By 10:00, little groups of friends were all over the room.
Most of them were gossiping and having a great time. It was
getting harder and harder to hear anything as the noise grew.
The sudden opening of the door brought the stillness of
stone.

In the doorway Miss Bigler, second in command under
Dr. Werner, drew herself up to full height. Her large frame
filled the space. Her unsmiling face, not softened by the black
hair swept behind in a bun, left no room for mistake. In some
ways Jeanmarie feared her more than Dr. Werner despite his
sternness. At least he was a known factor. Miss Bigler seemed
more like a storm waiting to erupt, but one wasn't sure when
or how.

"This is the way I want to hear you for the rest of today. Is
that clear?" Miss Bigler's tone was very clear, and the classroom silence was a definite unspoken "Yes, ma'am."

"May I see you a moment in the hallway, Miss Dove?" Miss
Bigler gestured to the hallway behind her. While the class
waited, making signs for fear that the door might open again,
Jeanmarie penciled a line through Miss Bigler's name on her
list of suspects to investigate. Miss Bigler would be one of
those who would die before breaking a rule, any rule, especially a government rule.

Miss Dove entered the room a little breathlessly. "My, oh my, class. I never would have guessed that our little old voices carried so far down this big old building, but they certainly do." She paused to smile then looked quite serious.

"I'm afraid I do have some bad news that Miss Bigler believes I ought to share with you." Now she did have everyone's attention. "As most of you know, Mrs. Gillpin's husband is a Navy man. I'm so sorry to announce that he was sorely wounded from an explosion on shipboard." Jeanmarie gasped. "However," Miss Dove continued, "the good news is that he is doing nicely. You all know Mrs. Gillpin will be gone for the week." Miss Dove looked longingly at the windows for a moment then back again. "It seems to me that you all are being called upon to show your patriotic spirit for the war cause this week. We'll just have to carry on and do our best until Mrs. Gillpin returns."

Nothing Miss Dove could have said or done would have reached most of the students, but with a single patriotic stroke she had done it. The reminder that Miss Bigler was still around may have helped, but nobody wanted to be called unpatriotic.

The news about Mr. Gillpin shocked the class. Most of the students would have defended Mrs. Gillpin against anyone outside the orphanage in spite of the hard times they sometimes gave her. Jeanmarie raised her hand.

"Please, Miss Dove," she asked, "was the ship sunk?"

"Oh, you mean Mr. Gillpin's ship," Miss Dove said, looking thoughtful for a moment. "No, no, I think it was just heavily damaged. Yes, that's what Miss Bigler said when she called late Monday night. The *S. S. McClellan* it was, just on its way out of port." Jeanmarie thanked her and turned an elated look on Pearl, who was looking at her with a puzzled expression. Quickly, Jeanmarie scribbled a note. "The *S. S. McClel-*

JEANMARIE and the FBI

lan was the ship with the name on it, the one on Mrs. G.'s map. I saw it Monday morning and so did Hans K."

In a moment Pearl slipped a small white piece of paper back to Jeanmarie. "Didn't Dr. Werner bring the letter on Friday, the one from the war office?" Werner had hand-delivered that letter shortly before noon just as the class was preparing to go to lunch. Jeanmarie read on—"Maybe Mr. G. told her the name of his ship and when it was leaving port? Werner could have opened it and resealed it, right?" Jeanmarie let the thought linger. The rest of the note was brief— "Or Banks . . . he could have seen it too; you said he was in her room."

Jeanmarie pictured Dr. Werner opening the letter, then making a call to his superiors. Someone must have told the Germans that the *McClellan* was about to sail. A submarine could have waited just off the coast and torpedoed her before she'd barely left the harbor. How else could the ship have been heavily damaged so close to port? Farmer Banks she dismissed from her mind. He was just an eccentric old man, certainly not the spy type. She couldn't imagine a spy without teeth.

Hans Koppel was a different story. He could have seen the map, even read the letter lying on the desk. But if he was the man who secretly delivered a package to Dr. Werner that night, how did it all tie together? Was Dr. Werner in cahoots with Hans? And how did the missing chickens fit in? The more she thought about Hans the more she wondered. He visited his mother two or three times a week, and he was single. What else did anyone really know about him? Under his name she penciled in a thick black line.

Her worries soon doubled. In the crowded cafeteria the gang sat huddled together, staring at the wrinkled paper Jeanmarie had just pulled from her lunch bag.

54

The drawing was crude but recognizable. "It's a key," Pearl whispered. "Somebody knows about the key, but who?"

Jeanmarie felt the skin of her scalp prickle. It had to be Emma. Leah must have reported what she'd overheard Luke say about the key. "It's Emma," she said. "She probably thinks we had something to do with stealing the missing chickens." One of them must have slipped the picture into her bag while it sat on the coatroom shelf.

Jeanmarie took charge. "We need to think what to do."

At the end of the table, Winnie squeezed in beside Tess. "Better fill me in quick on all the latest," she demanded.

"We've got to keep this to ourselves," Jeanmarie said. In a low voice she repeated all she knew about the mysterious picture of the key.

After a long silence, Winnie shook her head. "From what Leah heard they haven't much to go on. Luke could have meant any key to anything, including the kind you give a date to wear, honor society, and all that. Of course the stolen chickens complicates things. Still they don't have much that's solid, and they might not even connect the two." It was a long speech coming from Winnie, but it did hold out some comfort.

Pearl nodded in agreement. "She's right. If all of us stay quiet the whole thing could die down." She attacked her sandwich with new energy.

Maria was still skeptical. "Nobody can tell what Emma might do. If she does go to Mrs. Foster, and Foster reports it to Dr. Werner, the game's up." With the words her courage ebbed, and her voice faded to a small squeak.

From behind a hanky Winnie's muffled voice said, "At least the two of us are in the clear. We were at the movie the whole time, remember?"

At the thought, Maria's face brightened. The others glared at them. "Of course we'll all stick together no matter what," Maria added lamely.

"We have to," Jeanmarie pleaded. "We're all we've got. I mean each other, right?" The five of them had been as close as any family from Jeanmarie's first year at the orphanage.

Lunch was over, and Jeanmarie crumpled the picture and threw it into a trash container. The bell for class tolled as she ran back to the bench and picked up the newspaper left from the morning. Pearl's thin face lit up. "Thanks," she said. "I meant to ask if there were any extras." Then her eyes turned serious. "Listen, we don't dare go digging around that freezer anymore or anywhere else we're not supposed to be. Next week is Christmas." Pearl looked away from Jeanmarie, but not before Jeanmarie had seen a look of sadness sweep across her face. It was on Christmas Day that Pearl had been brought to the orphanage as an abandoned infant.

Jeanmarie stood still. "Listen, nothing will change Christmas Eve. It will be like old times. You bring the flashlight, and I'll bring the book." Her hand gripped Pearl's thin arm. "We'll have our Christmas by the furnace—just the two of us like always." Since Jeanmarie's first year at the orphanage, she and Pearl had spent every Christmas Eve together reading from Dickens's Christmas tale after everyone else was in bed asleep. It was their secret way of celebrating.

"I'll see to the flashlight, and there's apples for roasting still in the basket in the root cellar," Pearl said.

"Make that a Mickey for me," Jeanmarie said. Hot, half-burned potatoes called Mickeys, roasted illegally at the furnace or fireplace, were her favorites.

It was free reading time, and Jeanmarie spread the newspaper between her and Pearl. "FBI investigation leads to arrests of seven members of the American German Bund

Club," she read. "The FBI. I should have thought of it right away." Jeanmarie closed the paper. "All we have to do is write a letter telling them we think something is going on here that needs to be investigated," she said.

"But what proof do we have?" Pearl said. "If we go and name Dr. Werner or Hans Koppel the next thing you know somebody from the bureau is going to be out here asking questions of Werner, and we'll be in big trouble."

"Who says we have to name any names?" Jeanmarie took out a clean sheet of paper. "All we have to do is tell them there's been some suspicious goings-on here at the Apple Valley Orphanage, and we think it has something to do with the black market or passing on information to the enemy. That way we let them do the investigating. If we don't sign our names we'll be in the clear."

"Right," Pearl said. "It's the only way."

"You have the best handwriting," Jeanmarie said, placing the paper in front of Pearl.

The letter was finished, and Pearl added "Sincerely," then looked up at Jeanmarie. "How do you think we should sign it?" she asked.

Jeanmarie thought hard. "'Your obedient servants'? No, maybe 'Your friends'?" Nothing seemed quite right. How did one sign a letter to the FBI, especially when you couldn't give them your real name? "I know," she said. "We'll use false names, like some writers use pen names instead of their own. How about 'The Patriots'?"

"Great except for one thing," Pearl said, tapping the end of her pencil against her chin. "How are we supposed to get a letter back if they don't know where to send it?"

"We don't," Jeanmarie said. "All we do is keep an eye open for FBI agents suddenly popping up at the orphanage. Strangers, men in business suits, that kind of thing."

With a flourish Pearl signed "The Patriots," folded the letter, and put it in an envelope addressed to the FBI, Washington, D.C. "We can't mail this from here, so it will have to wait until one of us gets a pass off grounds," Jeanmarie said, tucking the letter into her pocket. Already she felt like a weight had been lifted off her shoulders. "We'll tell the others tonight after supper."

Maria, who had been darning a hole under the arm of her favorite sweater, looked up as Jeanmarie finished explaining about the letter. "We could all get passes on Saturday after work."

Tess frowned and pushed her reading glasses farther back on her nose. "I say let's do more than just mail the letter. We'll be off grounds anyway, so why not go ice skating at our private place?"

A sudden movement at the door startled them into silence. With a grin, Leah entered the room, picked up a magazine, and left, whistling.

Jeanmarie groaned. The small man-made lake on the grounds became a skating pond in winter for the orphanage kids, but for three winters the five of them had used a secret skating place all their own. They'd kept their skating pond a secret so far. How long had Leah been standing there?

"If she and Emma follow us and find out," Pearl whispered, "the whole world will know about our place."

"Worse," Jeanmarie stated flatly. "If they decide to tell Foster we'll be on restrictions the rest of the winter."

"Who says they have to find out?" Tess said. "I know a way . . ." Her voice became a whisper, and Jeanmarie leaned her head closer to listen.

SEVEN

A Mysterious Light

Jeanmarie tucked the off-ground pass for the five of them next to the letter to the FBI in her jacket pocket. Behind her a long line of kids still waited for Saturday passes from Dr. Werner. If all went well, the gang would be out of sight before anyone could follow them. They'd take the shortcut through the orchard to the crossroads, into the woods, then back onto the road to Gould's Camp. The camp was deserted in winter, its lake a large, private skating rink, and it was all theirs.

"Over here!" Tess called as Jeanmarie waved the pass in her mittened hand. "We hid the skates and a shovel to clear the ice by the old apple tree on the edge of the orchard," Tess said. "Last one there gets to carry the shovel." Jeanmarie and the others knew which tree Tess meant. It had been struck by lightning years before, and it looked like a giant Y, its center close enough to the ground for easy climbing.

The orchard ran along the road north of Wheelock. By the time Jeanmarie reached it, Tess stood at the tree waiting for the rest. Jeanmarie, whose mind had been on other things, came in last.

"The first one of you who makes a wisecrack better watch out," she threatened in a mock tone, brandishing the iron shovel borrowed from the cellar coal bin. The others grinned at her.

Winnie, whom no one would suspect of being a good runner though surprisingly she was, offered to carry Jeanmarie's skates.

"Fair's fair, Win, and I lost; besides, you've got enough to carry without my skates," Jeanmarie replied. Wherever Winnie went her backpack stuffed with all sorts of supplies went.

With skates across one shoulder and shovel on the other, Jeanmarie waded through snow undisturbed since the last snowfall and knee-high in places. Row on row of bare fruit trees, some old and gnarled, bushy with wild branches, others young and sticklike, stood in every direction. The orchard went on for acres and acres like a forest of trees with only the orderly rows to show that an orchard existed. Once past the first few rows it would shelter them from prying eyes, and at its entrance by the crossroads was a mailbox. Winter sun danced on the tree trunks and sparkled on the snow as they pushed on.

"In you go." Jeanmarie slipped the letter into the ancient mailbox. Ahead of them the road was clear, and they'd seen no one following them. Beyond this point and across the road the orchard ended and the real woods began. Here in spite of the lack of leaves, except for the brown ones still clinging to a few old oaks, the many trees, thick brush, and large rock outcrops on the uneven ground made good cover from the road. Jeanmarie threw down the shovel and re-arranged her skates.

Winnie seated herself on a snow-covered rock and wiped her face with a hanky.

Overhead a lone hawk circled in the gray sky. Wordlessly, Maria pointed toward it. In silence they watched until it was out of sight. "It must be great to have wings," Maria re-marked, straightening her cap. "Nothing to keep you from going anywhere you want, no rules, no passes needed." She sighed.

"Sure," Winnie, who was practical, chided, "but don't for-get that's a chicken hawk probably looking for food."

"Ugh," Maria retorted.

"Just natural," Jeanmarie added. "Come on; it's still two miles to Gould's." After a half hour of trudging through the snow, avoiding trees, and climbing small hills, they arrived at the dirt road leading to the camp.

In summer, Gould's was a campground for poor children from the city. Mr. Gould, a wealthy man, had donated the land and built cabins to house and feed the campers who filled the place with noise and laughter all summer long. Jeanmarie and the others often passed it on hikes. Over the stone arch entry into the camp was a large "No Trespassing" sign. The camp was private, but in winter it lay deserted.

Jeanmarie surveyed the scene before her with satisfac-tion. Empty cabins, padlocks on their doors, stood in clus-ters like spokes leading from the small lake. Deep woods lay behind the cabins. They were the only human beings in this world. She called "Hello-o-o," listening for her echo. Nothing stirred.

Maria, her dark eyes shining, spoke softly. "It's like having a whole planet to yourself, isn't it?" Then suddenly they were all running to the lake, whooping and hollering wildly in the freedom of their own place.

Hours later Jeanmarie sat at the edge of the pond; she loosened her skates and rubbed her cold feet. Cramped in last year's skates, her toes ached.

Beside her, Winnie dabbed at her runny nose. "I think Mr. Gould must be a wonderful man," she said, "to do all this for poor children."

"Well, for all we know, Winnie, you might be related to the great man," Maria said. "Any of us might, for that matter. Of course, not you, Jeanmarie. You've got a mother and a father."

Jeanmarie jerked on her boot. "Not that again," she said. "And sure, I've got a mother and a father, and look at me, I'm still here anyway."

Maria pursed her lips and turned away. Tess stood up, her square shoulders thrown back. "We're all still here too," she said. "Whoever our folks were is a secret that died with them."

Jeanmarie hunched her head down before she looked up. Her voice sounded small even to herself. "Sorry." She tied the laces of her skates together and fingered the knot. "I don't know what made me say that. Maybe it's because sometimes I wish things could be different. Having folks isn't always easy." Jeanmarie glanced at Pearl. "The letter that came for me the other day was from my mom. Things aren't so good. It's nothing new. I thought the arguing would stop once my father left." Swallowing hard she looked up. "Sometimes I think it would be better if I didn't know who he was."

"We're always talking about being rich folks' kids, but I guess I could be anybody's kid," Maria said softly. "Maybe it's better not to know."

Tess squatted down beside Jeanmarie. "You'd never guess it to look at your dad." She sat back on her heels, silent for a moment. "If you want, next time he visits, the rest of us can attack from behind a snow fort and pelt him with ice balls." Jeanmarie blinked hard and grinned. Tess extended a hand. "Friends, eh?" Jeanmarie gripped it tightly. Maria, then Pearl placed a hand on top of hers, and lastly Winnie.

"Thanks, gang," Jeanmarie said, swallowing hard.

They were halfway back to the orchard hill when Pearl asked, "Hey—where's the shovel?" All eyes looked at Jeanmarie.

"Beans!" she exclaimed. "Beans." The late afternoon was already turning to dusk, but she knew she would have to go back for the shovel. She wanted to be brave, tell them all to go on ahead without her, but the words stuck in her mouth. Without looking behind her, she hurried back toward the camp. For a minute she thought she was alone till she heard the sound of running feet thumping behind her.

The four waited at the gate while Jeanmarie ran lightly toward the pond to retrieve the shovel. As she bent to pick it up, she stopped, puzzled. In one of the small cabins directly within her line of vision was a light. Almost instantly it was gone. Picking up the shovel, she ran, looking behind her once at the cabins that now stood dark and silent in the cold. Someone or something had made that light appear and then disappear, but who or what? She didn't mention it to the others until they were safely away.

Too late to tramp through the orchard, they stuck to the main road instead. It wasn't likely anyone would spot them now, and the going was much easier on the plowed road.

Pearl looked thoughtful as Jeanmarie told of the light from the cabin. "Could be a tramp," she said. Jeanmarie nodded then stood still, horrified as Dr. Werner's car came around the curve in the road just ahead of them.

"Now we're in for it," Maria moaned as the black car pulled to a stop a foot from where they stood waiting.

"So, you skated too long, I see," Dr. Werner said with a wave of his hand toward the skates hanging from their shoulders. "Next time be careful to come back with the others or you will have no more passes until you learn to be punctual." With a nod of his head he dismissed them and drove away in the direction of town.

"At least he didn't ask where we'd been, or who with," Pearl said. "Funny, isn't it? Him being so easy on us, I mean. He must think we went skating on the old railroad pond past the orchard."

Jeanmarie looked at the car almost out of sight now. "It could be that he is too busy with something else to care about us, like he was the other day when he could have put me and Emma on restrictions for a month. Maybe he has something in the car and was in a hurry to deliver it."

"Like chickens?" Maria said. "Do you think he might be dealing with the black market?"

Jeanmarie pushed her wool hat to the back of her head. "It just dawns on me," she said, "that maybe the package from our mysterious stranger was a black-market item, that Werner never intended to put it in the freezer. We thought he was putting something in the freezer, but maybe he was taking something out—like boxes of chickens." She frowned. "So all that anger with Banks over the locker key was a front to cover his own tracks." She was still thinking furiously when a low moaning sound made her jump. All of them had heard it.

"Over there," Tess whispered. "I think it's coming from the observation tower." The tower, a box on giant spindly legs crisscrossed with ladder rungs, stood on the highest point of the orchard hill. It had been built for spotting enemy planes. Its base lay hidden behind a clump of thick, winter brush just off the road.

With her own heart beating loudly, Jeanmarie inched closer to the tower until she could see. It was Luke flat on his back, his arms flung out like a bird's wings. Even in the dimming light she could see how pale he looked. "Luke, what happened?" Jeanmarie cried, dropping the shovel and kneeling beside him in the snow. "Are you okay?"

Luke tried to sit up but groaned and lay back. "Dizzy," he moaned. "Must have fallen. Think I struck my head or something. Must have passed out." He closed his eyes then opened them to look at her, a dazed look on his face.

Pearl, who was kneeling at his other side, held up her mittened hand to the light. "Blood," she said. "I'll say you hit your head. Maybe you shouldn't try to move."

Jeanmarie was already stuffing her mittens close to Luke's head. Deftly she wadded up hats and mittens as fast as the girls passed them to her until a small layer of protection was between his exposed neck and the snow. While Tess and Maria ran for help, Pearl and Winnie held a hanky to Luke's wound. Jeanmarie chafed his hands then moved his feet onto her lap. "It won't be long, Luke, till someone comes. Tess and Maria are real runners," she said in her most hopeful voice. But even she was surprised when help came quicker than anyone could have guessed.

Tess was pulling, half-running beside Maria and a winded Farmer Banks. "What's this, what's this?" he said, coming to a stop beside Luke's prostrate body. "Had a fall, did you, boy?" he commented, lifting Luke's head with one of his large mittened hands. "Looks like a nasty cut, son. You must have struck something hard." With a strength that amazed Jeanmarie, the older man lifted Luke in his arms, hanging him like a sack of potatoes over his left shoulder. Luke groaned but made no protest.

"Coming back from town I was when the young ladies caught up with me," Mr. Banks said, breathing a little heavily under the load of Luke's weight. "Took the shortcut through the orchard; luck made me turn back onto the road. Would have missed you clean otherwise," he added.

At Dr. Werner's house, Mrs. Werner, an efficient little woman, took charge. Luke was laid on a couch with a pad and towels under his head while Farmer Banks went to telephone for the doctor. Mrs. Werner had no time for extras and firmly escorted the girls to the door closing it behind her.

Jeanmarie shrugged her shoulders. "Well, at least she'll call Mrs. Foster and explain what happened." As they walked the hill to Wheelock, Jeanmarie's foot sent a bit of hard-packed snow flying to the side of the road. "Funny," she said, "I wonder what Luke hit his head on. There wasn't a stone or a chunk of ice anywhere close to him and nothing under his head but snow."

Her instincts were up and searching for something, but what? "Tomorrow, I'm going back up to the tower and take a look," she announced.

"We'd better get back up there," Pearl said, her voice high with anxiety. "We left the shovel behind again." A chorus of groans rose in puffs of white breath. Mrs. Foster would be expecting them. The shovel would have to wait.

Jeanmarie sighed. She would think of something. Maybe she could fill up the coal buckets before the kitchen crew came downstairs in the morning so no one would even miss the shovel. The fellows who came to tend the big furnace always brought their own shovel so they were no problem.

In the kitchen, Mrs. Foster was just taking off her apron. "Well, that was Mrs. Werner on the phone. Might have known it would be you five who found the boy. Can't figure what you see in wandering about that orchard." Mrs. Foster was not given to long speeches. Abruptly, she went into the dining room leaving them to follow. Behind her, a smug-looking Emma turned to grin maliciously at Jeanmarie.

"At least they don't know about the shovel," whispered Winnie, holding a hanky to her nose.

Jeanmarie could feel drops of sweat on her forehead under her bangs as she stared at the list of chores posted on the wall behind the dining room door. Emma and Leah were on kitchen crew.

They would need the missing shovel to fill the coal scuttle!

Why hadn't she picked up the shovel along with her skates? Forgetting shovels seemed to be one of her faults. Maybe if she hadn't made them all go back for the thing that first time, they would have found Luke sooner. But then they would have missed Mr. Banks. Or would Dr. Werner have come along in time? Her head ached. Maybe she had one of Winnie's colds.

With a sigh she sat down at her place. Something hard, an odd shape, was on her chair. Quickly she fished it out. It was an iron key like the one in the lock of the large curio case in the living room. She could feel Emma's eyes boring into the back of her head from the table behind her, but she didn't turn around. Smiling grimly as if nothing had happened, she slipped the key under the edge of her plate. The key was meant as bait, but she wasn't going to walk into the trap. Ignoring it, she bowed her head for grace.

EIGHT

Unsolved Mysteries

On Sundays Mrs. Foster let the girls sleep an extra hour, but this morning Jeanmarie lay awake fully dressed under the covers. Mrs. Foster, still in her bathrobe, had barely disappeared back toward her rooms when Tess, whose bed was by the doorway, signaled the all clear. Darting like a cat, Jeanmarie was out the door and down the stairs before most of the others were out of bed. She had to do something about the missing shovel, but what she wasn't sure.

If Mike, the furnace man, came early maybe she could ask to borrow one of his shovels for the morning. But if Emma or Leah came down first to fill the kitchen coal scuttle, they would know the shovel was gone.

For a few minutes she stood warming herself by the giant furnace hoping for an inspiration. There was nothing in the fur-

68

nace room that even looked like a shovel. In one corner a broom and dustpan leaned against the stone wall. She picked up the dustpan and let it lie on her hand trying to judge the strength of its metal. Upstairs the cellar door opened.

Quickly she scooted into the coatroom and began to busy herself with her coat and boots.

"Move over; you're pushing me," a small, sleepy voice complained. It was Rosie trying to walk alongside Lizzie on the narrow cellar steps. The two little girls went on bumping their way down, holding an empty black coal bucket between them. With a leap, Jeanmarie was on the steps, finger to her lips, her left hand reaching for the heavy bucket.

"Hi," Lizzie whispered. "We have to fill up the bucket with coal for Emma and Leah, but we don't have to carry it back upstairs. Leah will," she said.

Jeanmarie didn't bother to say that the filled bucket would be too heavy for the two of them together to even lift. Speaking softly she led them into the furnace room. "By the looks of you, both of you need to comb your hair and wash your faces before you do anything else. Now if you don't say a word about this to Emma or Leah or anyone, I'll fill the bucket and leave it for Leah to find. Promise?"

Lizzie nodded her tangled red head of curls, and Rosie did the same.

"Was anybody in the kitchen when you came down?" Jeanmarie asked them.

Both girls answered at once. "Nope. Just us."

"Leah made us promise last night to get up early and come right down or else," Lizzie added, her eyes big with the seriousness of the or else part. "Nobody even saw us come down."

"Okay," Jeanmarie said, patting Lizzie's head reassuringly. "Up you go, and if they ask, just say that you finished the job. You have finished your part, so it isn't a lie." Smiling identical smiles each with two teeth missing near the front, the little girls turned and ran up the stairs.

With no time to spare, Jeanmarie picked up the dustpan, using it as a makeshift shovel in the coal bin. It was clumsy, but it worked. She shoveled at top speed ignoring coals that dropped on the concrete floor. It was taking too long; frustrated, she pushed the scuttle onto its side, using the pan to push in the coal. At last the thing was full. With her mittens in her hands just in case someone should see her leaving the cellar, she ran up the stairs.

No one had come down yet. In the upstairs hall, Leah, her back to Jeanmarie, bent to tie a shoelace. In sudden panic, Jeanmarie saw her blackened hands—smudged from the coal. Bunching her hands under her arms as if to warm them, she hurried past Leah into the bathroom kicking the door shut behind her.

Twenty minutes later she was on her way to chapel, no one the wiser about the missing shovel.

Tess fell into step with her. "You were right, Jeanmarie, about that old iron key you found last night. It fit into the curio case lock perfectly. I left it in the lock. A simple case of lost and found key."

"Good," Jeanmarie said in an equally low voice. "If we don't make anything of the key it will keep them guessing."

"Right," Pearl said. "By the way, I waited around the dining room until Leah went down for the coal bucket and watched her bring it up to the kitchen. All she said to Emma was, 'Here it is, nice and full.'" Jeanmarie nodded. They were in the clear for the moment.

The choir sang its Christmas carol and sat down in a crackle of starched surplices. Chaplain Stone, his glasses sliding down his nose, had begun to talk about licking one's problems, one of his favorite topics. True, he hadn't been chaplain very long at the orphanage, but Jeanmarie hadn't heard him talk about much else. Sighing, she turned her thoughts back to Christmas. Once she glanced up at Chaplain Stone. The heat in the chapel barely touched the chill air on cold days like today, but drops of sweat were running down the chaplain's face as he turned toward the choir. Surprised, she watched him mop his forehead with a handkerchief. When he turned away her mind wandered once more, this time to the shovel waiting in the orchard. They'd have to go back for it.

Outside Dr. Werner's office, the line waiting for passes to go for walks off the grounds seemed endless. Jeanmarie's turn finally came just as Irene came out waving her pass, her eyes lit with excitement. "Luke's coming home from the hospital in a day or two," she called out. "It's just a mild concussion, Dr. Werner says. Luke doesn't remember any of it. But he will be fine." Some of the boys standing nearby made good-natured jokes about a hard head. For a minute Jeanmarie envied Luke lying in the hospital with nurses to wait on him all day.

The shovel was where Jeanmarie had left it, on the ground near the tower base. She stood it upright in a snowbank and stared at the tower stairs, then at the spot where they'd found Luke. Pearl and the others were looking about, brushing the snow away from where Luke had lain and examining the ground carefully. "Nothing sharp so far!" Pearl called out.

Jeanmarie was puzzled. Where was the stone or whatever had cut Luke's head? "Let's climb up and give the tower a look," she said, making her way to the narrow ladder rungs that began at the base.

Maria and Winnie stayed below. Tess and Pearl followed her up the wooden ladder. It was easy at first, then tricky, and finally heady. "This is as high as I've ever climbed!" Tess exclaimed. There was just room enough for all three of them in the boxlike tower. Beyond them lay a little world spread out like a miniature map with curved roads and winter trees.

Carefully, Jeanmarie turned herself from north to east to south to west and north again. She could see where the road to town disappeared behind the orchard hill and wound its way to the horizon. Crossing it was the road that led to Gould Estates. From here one could even see the little woods and beyond to the side road that led to the camp entryway. There was nothing in the tower, no sign of blood where Luke might have banged his head before he fell.

In the distance, the blue and gray visitors' bus was making its way from town toward the orphanage. Jeanmarie's stomach sank. She'd almost forgotten that her father would be on it. "Guess I'll have to go back and meet the bus," she said.

"Don't worry," Pearl said firmly. "We'll be right close by if you need anything."

Winnie, who never had visitors, cheerfully volunteered to take the shovel back while the rest of them went to the gate to meet the bus.

As visitors stepped from Dr. Werner's office where they'd gone to register, Jeanmarie swallowed hard. Her father had come as usual. A dark-haired, handsome man, a bit short, he looked around warily then walked toward Jeanmarie, his shoulders hunched as if he carried a heavy burden.

He was the only visitor at Wheelock. In the living room he sat down heavily in an overstuffed chair. Jeanmarie sat on the sofa across from him.

"Got a kiss for your old man?" His voice was friendly and a little tired she thought. His blue eyes were unreadable. "Guess your ma told you I sort of lost my temper last week. I'm real sorry, and I promise you, kid, it won't ever happen again."

Dutifully she went to him, pecked his cheek, and scurried back to the sofa. In exactly two hours the visit would be over.

"Ain't much, but I got candy for you. Here, kid, take it." He held out a small shopping bag with the top of a net Christmas stocking sticking from it. She took it, muttering a thank-you that sounded more like she was choking.

"Hey, how about a little sandwich or something for your old man to eat. I ain't had anything yet, and my stomach's starting to sound like a rusty grinder. See what you can do, eh?"

Getting up from the sofa, she nodded, glad for the excuse to get away. She knew she could never ask Mrs. Foster for anything. She would have to take bread and jam and hope she didn't get caught. Fortunately, the kitchen was empty, and Mrs. Foster as usual was in her rooms. She found what she needed, then added three small leftover pickles along with a glass of milk.

She watched him eat, answering his questions about school and the holidays with the fewest number of words possible. She didn't mention the letter from her mother. When visiting time was up, she walked him to the bus, saw him climb aboard, and lifted a hand weakly in response to his wave. Why did he come at all? It was beyond her to figure out.

The candy-filled stocking was where she had left it on the living room floor. It was a thin red netting, the kind of thing one saw in the dime store at this time of year. She would put it under the tree for the little girls.

The tree, tall and wide with sweeping green branches, still smelled of the woods that lined the orphanage's west side where it had grown until a week ago. Jeanmarie hung the stocking on one of the upper branches and left.

At suppertime every eye turned to Mrs. Foster, who stood arms crossed over her massive bosom, feet solidly planted; she announced in a voice of doom, "Someone went into the refrigerator and deliberately stole three pickles. Those pickles belonged to me, not the institute but me personally. Now, whoever it was better speak up or you'll all be on restrictions the rest of the week."

Jeanmarie could feel her face getting hot. She couldn't bring herself to tell, but if she didn't they would all be on restrictions. No passes to town, no Christmas shopping, worse, no going to the Elks' Christmas party for the orphanage tomorrow night. Her mouth felt dry. Mrs. Foster was looking directly at her, a strange look as if she were trying to read her mind.

From the big girls' table the soft voice of Irene with a note of gentle laughter in it called out. "Oh, Mrs. Foster, I should have asked. We girls put those pickles into the potted meat sandwich mix along with the onion and celery for tomorrow night. I thought that was what you meant them for." Irene looked sweetly at Mrs. Foster.

Mrs. Foster faltered for a minute between ideas then let them drop. "Yes, well, let it go. Though three pickles in all that mix won't make much of a difference. Well, that's all, go on to your meal then, girls." Without saying more, Mrs. Foster retreated to her own table to eat in silence.

When they were alone, Jeanmarie looked solemnly at Irene. "I should have owned up. I guess I put you all in a tight spot." She wanted to say, "I made you lie," but she couldn't. Mother Anderson's preaching had been sternly clear about lying. It was a thing that tore at Jeanmarie's insides, making her face hot and her throat tight.

74

"So it was you, scamp," Irene said, tapping her on the nose lightly. "And you took two slices of bread. Lucky for you there was extra bread. You'd better be more careful from now on. If it's pickles you want, take a whole jar from the basement and don't leave any traces behind." She winked one beautiful eye and left.

Jeanmarie wanted to go after her and tell her she wouldn't do it again. Somehow she knew Irene wouldn't understand. True, she had stolen the pickles and the other things without giving it a thought, but in her heart she knew it was wrong, as wrong as lying. She couldn't confess to Mrs. Foster now. It would put Irene in trouble as well as herself. One thing she could do. She'd go without pickles the next three times they had them, even four. That ought to make up for something. She felt better now that that was settled.

There was no school in the morning, no work at the farmhouse, nothing but glorious freedom, and at the end of the week—Christmas Day. In her favorite spot on the living room floor behind a giant tiger plant, she drew out her lists of things to investigate and added "light at Gould's and FBI." So far none of them had seen anyone looking like an FBI agent at the orphanage. But then things like that took time.

On a blank sheet of paper she wrote down the unsolved mysteries: the stranger with an accent, Dr. Werner's package, missing chickens, the missing stone (or whatever hit Luke's head), the light in the deserted camp, Emma and Leah and the key, and fathers. The last item she crossed out after a minute of wondering why she had written it in the first place. Of course, fathers were a mystery in this place, even hers.

NINE

Footprints in the Snow

*I*t was sharply cold when the five of them started out for Gould's Camp. Jeanmarie shoved her pass deeper into her pocket and pulled on her heavy mittens. At least there were no skates or shovel to carry. This trip was strictly business. "I just can't figure it out," she said. "If we couldn't find anything Luke's head hit on, then what made him split his head?"

Pearl stopped walking and looked at her. "It's a mystery," she said. "He was pretty far from the ladder to have fallen from it, and anyway there was nothing but soft snow under him when we found him. Maybe somebody came from behind, struck him, and left. But who would do a thing like that and why?"

Maria looked dramatically at the others. "It could have been a tramp or a runaway from Letchfield who attacked Luke."

76

Once or twice a patient from Letchfield, a nearby hospital for the mentally ill, had escaped into the surrounding country-side. "But I don't see how anyone could have followed Luke up the ladder without Luke knowing it," she said.

Pearl bent down, drew a crude tower in the snow with a stick figure up in the tower. On the stairs she added another stick figure. Then she rubbed out both figures and drew one on the ground at the foot of the tower. "Didn't Irene say how lucky Luke was not to break a leg or something falling all that height?" She straightened and looked at the others whose faces were intent on hers. "What if Luke never climbed into the tower, but someone hit him on the head just as he was about to climb the steps?"

Jeanmarie was positive. "That's it. Luke suffered a mild concussion so he doesn't know if he fell from the ladder or not. He couldn't remember the details at all." She pushed her woolen cap behind her ears as she spoke. "I think some-body didn't want Luke to climb the tower that afternoon, but why and who?"

As they walked, Pearl said, "If it was a tramp, wouldn't he have taken Luke's boots or gloves or something? And when somebody escapes from Letchfield the authorities always warn people, so that can't be it. But," she went on, "suppose the person didn't want Luke to find something in the tower, or else he didn't want him to see something going on from up there." Pearl looked thoughtful. "Can't see why anybody'd leave anything in that old tower."

Maria's dark eyes brightened, making her face come alive. "So that leaves us with what somebody could see from up there. The road to town, or the road to the orphanage, or maybe the orchard itself."

"Or the road to Gould's," Jeanmarie added. She pictured the snow-covered orchard as she had seen it from the tower.

"There was nothing out of the ordinary in the orchard or the woods as far as I could see from the tower," she said. She remembered the way she'd watched the visitors' bus coming from town to the orphanage. But who would worry about a car or truck being seen on the road? Nothing added up.

"Maybe," she said, "Luke was knocked out because he was on duty looking for enemy planes. What if someone wanted to keep him from reporting an enemy plane?"

"But none of us saw anything, and what about Banks?" Tess asked.

They were no closer to a solution when they arrived at Gould's. Jeanmarie held up her hand for quiet. Before them the camp lay empty, asleep in the bright winter sun. And just how were they going to investigate a light in broad daylight?

"Why don't we split into teams," she suggested. "You three take the left side, and Pearl and I will take the right side. Look for signs of anything unusual." All three of Jeanmarie's cabins were padlocked, the windows boarded up. Besides their own footprints in the snow, there was no sign of anyone else having been there.

It was Winnie who made the discovery. Tess, her open jacket flapping about her, came running toward them. "You all better come," she said. "I think Winnie's found something."

By the cabin farthest from the lake and close to the woods, Maria and Winnie were peering into a chink of window left exposed beneath the boards. "You can just see in," Winnie said. "Over there against the wall is a pile of boxes, and there's a lantern on the table." She moved so Jeanmarie and the others could look.

Something about the packages seemed familiar to Jeanmarie. Where had she seen that white paper wrapping with the black numbers and letters like a code on them? The freezer! They were just like the boxes in the freezer. Except for the boxes and the table with the lantern, the cabin was deserted. The padlock on its door, a big old-fashioned lock, held firmly when she rattled it.

"If those aren't our boxes of stolen chicken, I'll eat my hat," Tess exclaimed. "I just bet that's what they are. Somebody is stashing black-market goods right here in Gould's." Like pieces of a puzzle, things were beginning to fit into a picture.

"If we could open the door or pry off some of the window boards, we could find out," Pearl said. "We can't ask Werner if he is mixed up in the black-market business. And if we go to the police, how will we prove that Werner is in on it?"

Jeanmarie nodded. They didn't have enough proof yet. "What we need is a plan and some hard evidence. We have to get inside this cabin." As she pulled on the old padlock, an idea flashed into her mind. "What about that big iron key to the curio case? If we're lucky, it will fit in this old lock. Two of us could go back and get it while the rest of us keep watch," she suggested. "Or one of us could go back for the key." She looked at Tess. Tess was the real athlete in the group. Nobody else could make it home and back in better time, and time was important.

As if she'd felt the unspoken message, Tess volunteered. With a nod she was off at a steady run.

Maria turned from watching her and pointed to the footprints they'd left by the cabin window and now right up to its door.

"What about our tracks? Whoever it is will figure somebody's on to them." It was true. Their tracks led right to the door of the cabin. A dead giveaway.

"Unless," Pearl said, "we make tracks at all the cabins. Then we can make prints down to the lake as if we'd gone skating. Like we're just kids out for fun."

"That ought to do," Jeanmarie agreed. "And we can cover some of the tracks by the window if we make it look like one of us fell down here and there."

"Right on," Maria cheered.

When Tess returned, breathing hard and holding the key in her hand, every cabin had footprints going to it and up and down its steps. Carefully stepping into her old tracks, Jeanmarie led the way up the end cabin's steps. She fit the key to the curio case into the padlock and it sprang open.

"We could be in big trouble breaking in like this," Winnie whispered.

For a minute Jeanmarie felt like a criminal. They were breaking into someone else's property. Dryness gripped her throat. Behind her, Maria made a choking sound. "Yes," Jeanmarie said, "but there's no time for anything else, and besides, it's the only way we can be sure." She pushed the door open wide. Cold air struck them. It was colder inside the cabin than outside. One of the packages was open, and Jeanmarie lifted the flaps. Under a piece of butcher paper was half a layer of chicken legs. Gingerly she touched the frozen meat.

Behind her Pearl whistled. "Whew, you guys were right—chicken thieves. From the looks of it somebody is running a black-market setup with our meat."

Jeanmarie replaced the paper and let the flaps slip back into place. "We'd better keep things exactly as we found them until we know more," she said. On the table next to a half-full lantern was a book of matches. She examined the cover, but the writing was too worn to tell her anything. There was nothing else in the cabin.

Maria pointed to her watch. "We better get going. What if whoever was here comes back and finds us snooping?"

The idea made Jeanmarie's stomach sink. "Right. Let's get out of here." She paused long enough to check the room once more. As Jeanmarie locked the padlock and pocketed the key, she gave a sigh of relief. No one had seen them in the cabin, and at last they had their first hard evidence!

"We still have to get back to the orchard before someone comes," Pearl said. Even with a pass the boundary lines for hiking off grounds stopped at the edge of the orchard.

Jeanmarie nodded. Her thoughts kept going over the discovery at Gould's. Every plan she thought of seemed to have one big hole—Dr. Werner. They still couldn't prove he was involved, but she knew they couldn't leave him out of the picture either.

Pearl said softly, "We'll just have to wait. If Werner is in this we'll find some way to trap him. Don't forget—tomorrow is Christmas Eve."

Pearl's voice held a deeper question and Jeanmarie nodded. "As of now everything else goes on hold for Christmas," she announced. "After all, even black marketers don't work on Christmas, right?" But did they? What if the chicken thieves decided to move on and take the evidence with them?

TEN

The Unexpected Gift

*I*n the morning thick flakes of snow poured down, covering the woods and the yard. The dorm window framed the scene outside as Jeanmarie and Maria watched. The orphanage buildings below the girls' hill were already hidden behind the thick curtain of blowing snow. It was as if Wheelock Cottage stood alone on the hill.

"It looks like one of those paperweights with the little villages inside that you turn upside down and the snowflakes float down, only thicker," Maria said.

Jeanmarie sighed. "Christmas Eve should always have snow." The spell of Christmas was on her. She felt like dancing, but instead she dove back onto her bed and thrust her cold feet under the blanket.

Maria and Pearl found space on each of the corners. Winnie sat on the foot of the bed, and Tess squeezed in next to her.

"What's this?" Irene asked, coming into the dorm. Her long, honey-wheat hair flowed past her shoulders, bright against the red sweater she wore. Maria slid to the floor to give Irene room on the crowded bed.

"No, thanks; I just want to tell you all that Luke is coming home today. He has to take it easy for a week, but he's okay." Irene's soft blue eyes glowed.

"Hey, that's great," Winnie said. "That means you'll get to see him tomorrow, I bet."

Irene's cheeks turned a delicate pink. "I have permission to walk over to Clark Cottage to visit. Right now shouldn't you lazy scamps get moving before you're late for breakfast? I'd better see you all downstairs, and on time," she said, as someone called her from the hallway.

"I suppose the two of them will marry as soon as Irene turns eighteen and gets out of here," Maria said with a dreamy look in her eyes.

"Maybe," Jeanmarie said, "if he doesn't get killed first."

"Who'd want to hurt Luke?" Maria's dark eyes flashed.

"Are you forgetting somebody already tried?" Pearl said. "It could have been a lot worse than a concussion, you know. He might have died if we hadn't found him." Jeanmarie nodded. The whole problem of Luke, Dr. Werner, and the chickens they'd found in the cabin seemed suddenly more dangerous and important than any of them had dreamed. "And another thing," she said. "I'm thinking Christmas might be just the cover whoever's in this chicken-stealing ring will use to strike again. We'll have to keep a watch starting with Werner, his house, where he goes."

Pearl looked at Jeanmarie and shook her head. "Didn't somebody around here say let's put this whole business away for one day?"

Jeanmarie groaned. "I know I did, but it just won't stay put."

"I can keep a lookout," Winnie volunteered, "after I finish cleaning the kitchen pots." Between them they divided the watch. Jeanmarie's would be from 1:00 until 3:00 P.M.

By evening the snow had stopped. Jeanmarie took a last look under the Christmas tree, its branches thick with popcorn strings, cranberry ropes, and dozens of paper ornaments the girls had made. From the lower branches Lizzie's and Rosie's paper snowflakes danced merrily next to a blizzard of paper stars. Except for Winnie and Leah, there were extra gifts for all the girls. Two were addressed to Jeanmarie from her mom. One flat package wrapped in a paper napkin had a printed tag that said, "For Jeenmaree." Jeanmarie smiled, guessing already the carefully colored pictures inside it from Lizzie and the others.

She placed some small packages she'd been saving for Winnie near the one from the orphanage. She was about to leave when her glance fell on two packages for Emma. Nearby was a small box wrapped in telltale institute paper for Leah. Jeanmarie recognized the shape of the box—a hairbrush. But Leah already had a good hairbrush; she'd seen it. Someone had made a mistake. There were no other packages for Leah under the tree. Suddenly an idea took hold of her. She ran out of the room and up the stairs.

From under her bed she fished out her strongbox. Inside lay a new pencil sharpener in the shape of a tiny wishing well. It was heavy, some kind of shiny metal with a brightly painted handle and bucket. Quickly she took it out and wrapped it in a paper napkin. Lavishly she added three new pencils from her school supply and a new eraser. Would it be going too far to add one of her precious notebooks? Hesitating slightly, she lifted a small, blue-covered pad and added it to the gift, then wrapped the bundle with some leftover paper. It was a bulky package when she finished but brightly wrapped and quite Christmasy. A small bit of paper did for a tag. On it she printed: TO LEAH, LOVE SANTA. Satisfied, she stuck the package under her sweater. A feeling like warm energy, the kind she always felt with a good secret, filled her.

On the stairs, heading the other way, Emma passed her, a smug look on her face. Jeanmarie wondered what was up but put it out of her mind. The living room was still deserted, and gently she pushed the new present under a branch with a small red star on its needles.

She was so absorbed that the unexpected rapping on the living room window next to the tree startled her. "What!" she exclaimed. Someone outside was knocking insistently on the frosted glass. With her face pressed close to the cold glass, Jeanmarie made out a heavily muffled Maria gesturing with her flashlight. There was no mistaking her frantic signals. Nodding that she understood, Jeanmarie ran to grab her coat and quietly let herself out of the cellar door.

The night air was turning bitterly cold. Maria met her at the corner of the house. "What is it? What's going on?" Jeanmarie was already shivering. "Why didn't you just come inside and warm up a minute?" she asked.

"Can't," Maria muttered through the woolen scarf tied about the lower part of her face. "It's Werner, and I think we've got him. You better come."

Jeanmarie pulled up her own hood. "Where is he? What's happening?"

Maria led her toward the south side of the house. In the dark without the lamplight from the road, the windows behind them were like warm yellow beacons in the night. "Looks like a meeting again, only down at the edge of the woods near Werner's house," Maria said. "Pearl's watching them."

Jeanmarie gripped Maria's arm. "Good work; let's go." They approached through the woods, crouching and moving silently from cover to cover. Jeanmarie could hear her heart beating loudly.

Near the Werners' house where the undergrowth was still thick and bushy, Pearl huddled, a small dark shape close against a large rock. Just beyond, the land sloped gradually down to the road. In the bright headlights reflecting on the snow, Dr. Werner stood close to a small delivery truck.

"Well, Gustav," Werner's voice carried clearly, "I am indebted to you. This war is a crazy business." Jeanmarie could not hear the person in the truck. "The meat is good," Werner said next. "Better get home to your own Christmas, man." As Werner stood back to watch the truck leave, Jeanmarie flattened herself to the ground, Pearl and Maria crouched next to her.

For a long while they waited, cold and stiff, but not daring to move. In the distance a door slammed. "That's it," Maria whispered. "Werner's gone in." She stood half-bent to look, then straightened up.

"Well, that settles it," Jeanmarie stated emphatically. "Werner is in on the black-market ring. Gustav, whoever he is, must be the one picking up the meat. Dr. Werner is our man alright." All they had to do now was find evidence on him that the police would believe.

Pearl stood up, rubbing her legs to warm them. "It's a clever scheme. Dr. Werner hires somebody to pick up the meat and hide it at Gould's, then when they're ready, they sell. Probably takes some for himself too. Maybe he gets an exchange like beef for himself—could've been beef in that first package."

"Right," Jeanmarie said. "It fits with what we saw the first time and with that note from Werner's desk." Jeanmarie picked her way between last year's withered bushes feeling the cold inside her mittens. "As soon as Christmas is over we'll have to set a trap and catch him red-handed."

"Sure," Pearl agreed, "but how?"

Jeanmarie had no idea yet. Aloud she said, "Well, there's always Wilfred. He might be able to help us." She didn't say how. But Wilfred could be trusted, and his brain was awesome. If anyone could think of something it would be Wilfred. Besides, if they were going back to Gould's she liked the idea of Wilfred going along with them. And she knew that she was going back. Just as soon as Christmas was over.

As they reached the top of the hill, Jeanmarie glanced down the road toward the gym and Dr. Werner's house. Someone was out walking. She could tell by the light swinging from side to side that whoever it was seemed to zigzag first to one side of the road, then to the other. Listening, she thought she heard singing.

"Chaplain Stone," Maria whispered. It was the chaplain again, keeping company with himself and on Christmas Eve too.

"Doesn't he ever go home?" Jeanmarie said. Turning, she hurried toward the friendly light coming from the cottage windows. She had one more meeting to make tonight.

This was really Christmas Eve, the way it should be. Across from Jeanmarie Pearl threw an apple core into the open furnace door.

"You want another apple?" Pearl asked holding out a small wizened, brown-skinned apple.

"No thanks, can't eat another bite." Jeanmarie added a handful of blackened Mickey skins to the fire. It had all been perfect. They had finished the Christmas story, eaten, and watched the fire dance in the furnace. Pearl's soft brown eyes glowed, her face red from bending too close to the fire. It was time to go upstairs before it got too late.

"Merry Christmas," Jeanmarie said, sticking her arms into her sweater, its sleeves warm from hanging next to the furnace.

"Merry Christmas," Pearl returned. "Till next year," she added.

"And the next and the next," Jeanmarie said, holding Charles Dickens's *A Christmas Carol* against her chest. This was the third year they'd read it together in their own private Christmas Eve celebration. It had become their best secret, a part of Christmas she knew they'd never give up.

"You go first," Pearl said. "I'll follow."

Jeanmarie nodded. It would be safer that way. She went quickly up the stairs and slipped into the kitchen. Nothing stirred except for a hissing coal in the stove and the loud ticking of the kitchen clock on the wall. Mrs. Foster was up in her own rooms as always, and the rest of the girls were tucked safely in their beds.

Christmas morning dawned in a fresh, heavy, unrelenting snowstorm. Mrs. Foster's grace was extra long at breakfast, but Jeanmarie didn't mind, especially since they were having her favorite treat—grapefruit halves drenched with honey that had stood all night soaking deep into the yellow fruit. She was feeling so generous this morning that she smiled at everyone, even Leah sitting two tables away. Leah grinned back—an uncomfortable kind of grin—and Jeanmarie looked in another direction.

Gift opening was partly a surprise and partly expected. Every girl already knew what gifts for under one dollar she had chosen from the orphanage, but there was always the surprise of which one of the two choices it was. Jeanmarie had asked for a hairbrush. It was a pink-handled one with good firm bristles.

Unwrapping the gifts from her mom was fun. In the first box lay a soft pink sweater and in the second a matching skirt.

"Beautiful," Tess said, looking up from examining the new wide bracelet on her arm.

Jeanmarie laughed and picked up a gift she hadn't noticed until Maria pointed it out to her. It was a small box wrapped in white tissue with her name on it. She opened it carefully. Trying to keep as much of the tissue from tearing as she could, she lifted the lid. "What?" was all she could say. Inside the box lay a large iron key exactly like the one to the curio cabinet. This time tears threatened to spill from her eyes, and they were not the sad kind. Looking up she caught Leah staring at her. At her side Emma was grinning. In Leah's lap lay the small wishing well, the pencils, the eraser, and the blue notebook. Jeanmarie felt a hard lump in her throat, shoved the small box on top of her new sweater, and left quickly.

ELEVEN

A Midnight Walk

Jeanmarie held her hands out toward the flames dancing in the great old fireplace that took up most of one wall of the living room. Built in the days when fireplaces were huge, it held a fat log that blazed merrily. The dark wood mantel high above it sprouted a garden of holly and ivy with red berries shining among the greens. At each end the girls had fastened red velvet bows. Maria lay sprawled on the rug nearby. Tess, Winnie, and Pearl had divided the couch among them. Winnie was already snoring gently. The little girls were playing house in their dorm room, and Leah and Emma were upstairs with the older girls, styling hair. Mrs. Foster, as usual, was in her room.

Outside another storm spilled snow that swirled in the wind like dancers on spiral staircases. Jeanmarie threw the core of a roasted apple into the fire where it hissed for a second then disappeared. The shriveled apples wintering in baskets down in the fruit cellar were too leathery to eat without roasting first on the coals. Blackened on the outside their warm insides were soft and delicious. She didn't stop to worry that they had taken the apples without permission, not on Christmas Day.

The snow was filling the windowpanes like half-closed, white shutters, making the room within a snug, warm little world.

Jeanmarie could feel her eyes drooping.

How long she slept she didn't know, but all of them seemed to wake up at the same time. Small flames licked the last bits of blackened wood, and darkness had fallen outside. Jeanmarie stood up to stretch, her arms and legs still tingling from where she'd pressed against the hard floor as she slept.

"Oh boy, none of us will want to sleep tonight," Winnie said, rubbing her eyes. "It must have been the apples." She had eaten three.

Tess, who was doing pushups on the floor, stopped and sat up. "Maybe we shouldn't waste the night sleeping. Let's think of something we could do," she said. "Tomorrow is a free day, in fact the whole week is free."

Jeanmarie sat down cross-legged next to Tess, motioning the others to join them. She held up one slender hand for silence and lowered her voice to a whisper. "It's snowed all day, right? So the way I figure it, nobody is going to be traveling outside tonight, right?" Heads nodded in agreement. "I say it's the perfect time to set our trap for Werner." No one moved or said anything. She could see that it would take some talking to convince the group.

It was as if her words came by themselves, fitting into the plan forming in her mind. She heard herself say, "We can be at Gould's in an hour, back before anyone knows we went, and all snug in our beds. There's not a single house between here and Gould's, and besides, no one will be on the roads tonight anyway." Jeanmarie saw that they were listening, listening intently.

"All the packages in the locker were marked, right? So all we have to do is take some of the packages stored in the cabin and let the police match up the markings. We tell them what we know and let them set up the rest to catch Werner at a delivery." She paused to let the group think for a minute.

A spark of interest had come into Pearl's eyes. "Maybe you're on to something," she said. "I mean, it might work. If we could grab the packages, stash them somewhere safe, and do it all between midnight and 3:00 A.M., nobody would know. We could call the police and tell them to watch Werner and where to find the packages. We won't even have to give our names."

Maria grinned, making a small dimple appear below the beauty mark on the left side of her face. "Remember the time we all went out on the summer porch to sleep after everyone else was dead to the world?" She didn't remind them they'd been caught after only an hour of enjoying the cool air because Mrs. Foster had come out to take in the air too. All of them had been on restrictions for two weeks. "I reckon we could do this if we wanted to," she added.

Winnie pursed her lips for a moment before she spoke. "Well, it would be cold, but I suppose we could dress for it. We'd just put on our clothes over our night things anyway."

Jeanmarie smiled. "You can have my brown wool sweater for an extra layer, Win. We're agreed then to go tonight?" She looked around the group as each girl solemnly nodded. "Okay. The next thing we need to do is decide on where to hide the packages. How about the old migrant house?"

At exactly midnight, Jeanmarie's inner clock woke her. Barefoot so as to make no sound, she went from bed to bed gently shaking the others. Maria was already awake. Winnie rolled over twice before she finally sat up. Tess started to speak, but Jeanmarie quickly put her hand over her mouth stifling the sound. Pearl had slipped like a shadow down the hall, past the closed door to the other dorm, and toward the stairs. Every squeak of the wooden stairs brought a moment of stabbing fear, but finally they'd reached the cellar in safety, and Jeanmarie let out a deep breath.

With the door above the cellar stairs closed they were two floors away from the sleeping household. Shut away in the windowless cellar they could light flashlights. Jeanmarie dressed quickly, pulling her scarf over her mouth. It was half-past twelve on her watch as they finally left by the cellar door, its rusty lock all but useless.

The snow had stopped, but a heavy darkness covered the moonless, starless night. It really had snowed hard. At least a foot of snow made every step work. Jeanmarie cupped her flashlight in her mittened hands playing it in front of them straight ahead in the direction where she knew the orchard would be. Tess kept hers pointed down as they trudged side by side along what should have been the road in back of the house. Pearl and Winnie followed, trying to step in the broken path ahead of them. Nobody spoke till they reached the first line of orchard trees.

Jeanmarie pulled her scarf down to her chin. It was warm and moist where it covered her mouth, and for a few seconds the cold air felt good. She let her light flash up and down the nearest tree. Even in the dark with snow heavy on its branches, she was sure which tree this was. It was a smaller one, right on the edge of where the road now hidden under snow must be. Jeanmarie knew the shape, the size, the exact location of every one of the border trees, having raided them each summer and fall faithfully. The biggest, oldest tree was the first one on the narrow road leading through the heart of the orchard. It still bore apples though they weren't quite as good as those on the younger trees. Slowly she led the group to the right. "There, over there's the old tree and the road," she called, the wind flinging her words sideways.

She steered them close to the line of trees on the right that marked the road. Soon they should come to the deserted house where the migrant workers stayed during harvest.

As if in answer, the snow-topped fence posts bordering the old two-story frame house appeared in the weak light of the flashlight. She could see little of the rest of the house. No one lived in the place except during apple picking time, but even empty, an eerie sense of its presence loomed over her. No one spoke until they were well away from the place.

At the crossroad where the orchard ended and the road to Gould's began, they stopped to rest. Tess played her light over the group huddling close to each other and laughed nervously.

All of them were muffled to the teeth, barely recognizable. "This has got to be our craziest stunt," she said. "At least, I don't think there is another human being out tonight."

Pearl sniffed behind her scarf. "I don't mind that in the least," she said. "All I want is for it to stay that way, nobody else between here and home but us."

Maria slapped her arms against her body to keep warm, and at her side Winnie did a little jig to keep her feet moving. Suddenly they both stopped still. Something huge and dark had swooped close above their heads. For a second or two nobody moved, then Tess played her light above them into the trees. In the branches two yellow eyes stared back.

"An owl," Maria screeched. The large bird, barely discernible on its perch, didn't move.

"It's just an old bird," Winnie said soothingly. "He probably thinks we're out looking for our dinner the way he is." She raised one arm toward the bird, and without a sound it flew off into the darkness.

Jeanmarie turned in the direction of the road. "We'd better get on our way before all of us freeze," she cautioned. Here the trees thinned, and bushy undergrowth bordered the road most of the way to Gould's. A sharp, cold wind continued to blow against them, and ahead of the rest she felt its full impact. Even with her head lowered her face stung where her eyes showed between the scarf and cap pulled low on her forehead. She gritted her teeth, pulled the cap down further, and pushed on.

It seemed to Jeanmarie that hours had gone by when she stumbled against the gateposts to Gould's. She pointed the flashlight at her watch; it said 1:30.

Next to her Winnie groaned. "I knew I should have stayed in bed."

"Listen," Jeanmarie warned. In the stillness all of them listened. Except for the howling wind nothing else besides themselves seemed abroad. Ahead of them the camp lay wrapped in darkness. In her jacket pocket lay the iron key to unlock the cabin.

"Okay, it looks good so far," Jeanmarie whispered. "All we have to do is get into the cabin, grab the packages, and back we go."

In spite of the layers of clothing and jacket she could hear her heart beating. What if someone was asleep in the cabin? What if the packages were gone and she had led them all on a wild goose chase? That would be worse almost than the first thought, though the idea of a stranger, maybe a thug, didn't appeal to her either. With a show of bravado she started toward the cabins.

Behind her the others moved in close. Tess, switching off her flashlight, stepped beside Jeanmarie.

Without warning, out of the dark ahead came the barking of a dog. Tess clutched Jeanmarie's arm, knocking the flashlight to the ground. Before either of them could say a word, the door of the farthest cabin opened, sending a gleam of yellow light a little way into the night before the dark swallowed it. A shape stood outlined in the doorway. From this distance it was impossible to see more.

The girls froze. Fortunately, Jeanmarie's light lay face down under the snow. She didn't dare pick it up or move. In a minute she knew she would turn and run.

From somewhere behind the figure in the doorway came the growl of a dog, fierce, terrifying. It continued growling, low-throated harsh sounds until the figure said something.

Jeanmarie couldn't hear the words. "Please, dear God, don't let that dog come after us," she prayed silently. A moment later the door closed, shutting away the light. Jeanmarie's legs trembled. For a few seconds all of them stood still before they turned and ran. Jeanmarie grabbed up her flashlight and ran back through the entryway. From behind her the barking began again then stopped abruptly. Tess was beside her, and even Winnie seemed to have found new strength to run. "Keep going," Jeanmarie said between her teeth. "Don't stop." Her chest felt as if it would explode.

They were into the trees now at the edge of the road, and Jeanmarie could go no farther. Next to her Tess gasped for breath. Outside of their own labored breathing and the wind, the night seemed still. There was no sign of pursuit.

Breathing hard, Tess turned to Jeanmarie. "I think it's okay. I don't think anybody's coming. The dog would have been here by now. Anyway, there goes our plan."

In the dark beside her Pearl agreed. "Right. So let's get out of here. Whoever is in there must be part of the ring."

Jeanmarie turned her flashlight on, playing it over the trees where they stood. "We better go back on the road. We can spot anyone coming, and it will be a lot easier walking than in here." She linked an arm with Winnie who groaned. "Come on, old thing, we'll make it." Jeanmarie hoped her voice sounded better than she felt. At least it wasn't snowing. Suddenly she groaned. That meant tomorrow whoever was in the cabin would see their tracks in the snow. There was only one thing left to do.

"I know this will sound crazy," she said, "but it's the only thing we can do to cover our tracks. We've got to leave a trail straight to the migrant workers' place. That way it will look like we were just a bunch of tramps looking for a place to stay at Gould's and ran when the dog barked. They'll think we made for the old orchard house."

"Listen," Tess argued, "when I said let's do something tonight I didn't mean to get us killed. Just what do we do if somebody is really holed up at the migrants' place?"

Jeanmarie plunged ahead. "We passed it before, didn't we? We've been by it half a dozen times this winter, and so has Luke and anyone else who went to the watchtower. No smart tramp would stay there, but with our tracks it will look like someone did."

Jeanmarie no longer felt tired. The wind pushed at them from behind like a cold hand. When they reached the dark, deserted house she let her light search over its snow-covered steps, its silent door. Gritting her teeth, she climbed the steps.

"You aren't really going in there," Maria whispered from behind her.

Jeanmarie turned to explain, her own voice hushed. "We have to get inside and make it look like someone was here." Carefully she pressed against the wooden door, and it opened. A step at a time she made her way inside holding the light straight before her then turning it to explore the corners, the walls, even the ceiling of the room. It was bare, cold, and ugly. Strips of old wallpaper hung from the walls, and drifts of dirt, old cans, and paper lay strewn on the floor.

"Ugh," Winnie said. "It looks like something out of a war movie. How could anyone live here?"

"Okay," Pearl said in a matter-of-fact voice. "We did what we came for, now let's go." She started for the door.

"Wait a minute," Jeanmarie commanded. "There's one thing more. We can't just walk out of here and leave a trail right to our cellar door." Maria groaned, and Pearl muttered, "I knew there would be a hitch just when we're almost home."

"Look," Jeanmarie said trying to sound confident, "all we have to do is stay in the orchard until we hit the road by Wheelock. We'll find our original tracks and walk backwards in them to the house." There was a dead silence.

By the time they reached the edge of the orchard, Jeanmarie could no longer feel the throbbing of her legs or the ache in her arm. The flashlight had grown to a dead weight as she fought to keep it pointing ahead.

It was Tess's light that found the tracks they had left earlier, still visible across the yard. Jeanmarie led the way, walking backwards one step at a time like a robot, until she stumbled against the cellar door.

Down the cellar steps, into the warm furnace room, and back to the coat hooks she led them, too tired for words. It was almost 3:30 by her watch. It had taken them twice as long coming back.

At the foot of the cellar stairs Winnie sneezed. Jeanmarie giggled, and then she was laughing and trying to stifle the sounds with the back of her sleeve. Next to her Tess clung to the railing, her body contorted in laughter. Pearl had collapsed on the floor, holding her sides and choking on muffled gasps.

Tears streamed down Jeanmarie's face, and her sides ached when the fit finally subsided. She had no idea what they were laughing at. Drying her eyes, Winnie, who had begun it all, pointed to the upstairs door. Jeanmarie nodded and wiped her wet face with the back of her hand. A chilling reality began to set in—they were not safe yet.

Once the stairs creaked under somebody's weight, and Jeanmarie's spine tingled as she listened for a sign of Mrs. Foster or worse, Emma or Leah.

Jeanmarie's bed stood farthest from the door. Numbly she fell into it, pulled the covers around her, and closed her eyes.

TWELVE

The Plan

Somebody was shaking her, calling "Jeanmarie." Didn't they know that she couldn't open her eyes, not yet. Suddenly cold trickled across her face and down between her neck and nightgown. She twisted away, her eyes open wide. "Stop it!" she sputtered, wiping drops of water from her face.

Above her Pearl stood, fully dressed, a cup in her hand. "Sorry, but you just wouldn't wake up, and in five minutes you'll be late to breakfast." Pearl looked awful; dark circles under her brown eyes made them look huge and black in her thin face.

Jeanmarie nodded. "Okay, okay, I'm up." She pushed off the covers and stood, falling back immediately onto the bed. "Oh, Pearl, I feel like I'll never be the same." Her legs, her whole body wanted nothing more than to stay in bed for hours, maybe a whole day.

Pearl took her arm and helped her up. "I know it, but you can't give in. Come on now, here's your stuff; get dressed, please." She held out Jeanmarie's clothes, not moving till each piece was taken and put on.

Pearl was right. Unless you were sick there was no staying in bed, and if you were sick you would have to see the nurse. Without a temperature you would be pronounced "well." Jeanmarie stumbled along behind Pearl to the dining room. The others were already seated, waiting for grace as the two of them slipped into their seats. Mrs. Foster droned on, stopping just as Jeanmarie felt herself sinking into sleep.

"Eat," Tess commanded. All of them ate, paying attention for the moment to the bowls of hot cereal in front of them. There was apple butter this morning and buttered toast. Under Tess's watchful eye, Jeanmarie ate everything without tasting any of it, but her mind was beginning to clear as she finished the last bite.

Across from her Pearl and Maria looked as if they'd just ended the day instead of begun it. Silently, mechanically, they cleared their plates under Tess's continual prodding. Tess seemed most awake. Jeanmarie yawned. Her eyelids drooped, and the room felt stuffy.

Pearl pushed her bangs back from her forehead, exposing a patch of brown freckles, and in a low voice said, "Listen, I've been thinking. This is vacation week. Why don't we spend the rest of the morning in the living room with a board game, and that way we can get some sleep. The others will be in the playroom, and we'd have the whole living room to ourselves." During the Christmas week holiday the small playroom was where the younger girls liked to play. Leah and Emma would likely take command of the radio at the opposite end of the room where the young ones set up their games and spend the morning there.

"Good thinking," Jeanmarie murmured. "I don't know how long I can stay awake." The rules were strict—no one was allowed to sleep or even rest on the beds during the day. A Monopoly game on the living room floor was their best hope for a cover-up.

By 9:30 the house was quiet. Mrs. Foster was up in her own rooms. Maria dealt the money, set up the board, and called loudly, "Your turn, Pearl!" Pearl was already asleep on her stomach, her face hidden in the crook of one arm resting on her pile of cards. Jeanmarie knew nothing more till she heard May's voice calling, "Hey, you sleepyheads, it's time for lunch." Lunch! It was nearly noon by her watch. Quickly she woke the others.

The afternoon mail brought another letter marked Miss Jeanmarie Crew. She recognized the handwriting as her mother's. Her mother didn't write often, and this was the second one this month. Alone in the dorm room she opened it, skimming quickly to find whatever it was that had made her mother write again so soon.

You need to know that I am now living in a dormitory for the women factory workers here. It's not the Ritz, but it's got beds and things like blankets, soap, and towels. The trouble is the factories can't get enough workers now that the men are mostly off to the war. So they pay us women to come and give us a place to stay in the dormitory. As I say, the place is crowded, and half the time you have to stand in line for the showers, but it isn't too bad.

The letter went on to give an address in New Jersey. Jeanmarie folded it back into its creases and tucked it into her box.

Her father would ask her next time he came if she knew where her mother was. She wouldn't memorize the address. She would say she didn't know the address, and she didn't, not by heart. She pictured her mother standing in line for the showers, her red-brown hair piled up on her head. Standing in line for things at the orphanage was something she knew about. Smiling, she pulled the spread on her bed to straighten its wrinkles. She looked up to find Pearl standing in the doorway watching her.

"You okay?" Pearl asked.

"A-OK, old buddy, and I think I've got a plan for us." Jeanmarie picked up her lists and grinned.

"Oh no. Not after last night. This had better be good," Pearl said. Beside her Tess and Maria groaned, and Winnie looked grim.

Seated in a semicircle in a corner of the bedroom away from eavesdroppers, Jeanmarie laid out her plan. "You heard Mrs. Foster announce that Dr. Werner's office would be open from 12:30 to 1:00 tomorrow afternoon for passes."

"Not Gould's again," Pearl said.

"No way," Maria added firmly. "Whoever was in that cabin might still be there."

Jeanmarie raised her hand for silence. "But that's it. In the daytime we'll just be a bunch of kids coming to skate. If somebody is there, we pretend innocence. If not, then we move in, take the package, and move out." She hoped no one would ask why they hadn't waited last night and gone in the daylight. "At least now we know there was someone in the cabin," she added, "and we aren't going in blindly."

"What about it, Maria?" Jeanmarie asked looking straight into her dark eyes.

"I don't know. I don't know about that dog." She shook her head as if to clear it. "If it's a guard dog, one of those big police dogs, we could be in trouble."

"We could ask Wilfred to go too," Jeanmarie said quietly. "You know how he is with dogs." Not only was Wilfred the brain of the school but he had a way with animals, all kinds, and especially dogs. Everybody brought him the wounded birds they found, or sick cats, even abandoned baby mice. Dogs who found their way onto the institute grounds would go to him over anyone else. The animals seemed to know something about Wilfred that none of the rest of them knew.

"Wilfred might be useful if the dog is still there," Maria said thoughtfully.

"Agreed?" Jeanmarie asked. No one was enthusiastic, but heads nodded and she went on. "Then all we have to do is convince Wilfred." But how? Jeanmarie pursed her lips. It was too risky to try walking up the boys' hill to Grant Cottage. Getting caught meant restrictions for sure.

Irene's clear soprano voice came floating in from the hallway. "Irene, that's it." Jeanmarie struggled to her feet and called, "Irene, can you spare a minute?"

Irene stood framed in the doorway, a vision of pink and white, her long, honey-wheat hair streaming over a soft pink sweater. "What's up?" she asked, coming to sit by the group.

Jeanmarie sat down again smiling. "Well, we were wondering—if you're going over to see Luke, could you take a note for Wilfred? Since they both live in Grant Cottage maybe Luke could pass the note on to Wilfred." She stopped and waited respectfully for Irene's answer.

Irene reached out a slender hand to tug on Jeanmarie's braided hair. "What am I getting myself into?" she asked.

"Nothing much," Jeanmarie said quickly. "Just a note to invite Wilfred on a walk. Werner's giving out passes tomorrow." She grinned hopefully. "You know Wilfred, the class brain. We need him for a little project."

Irene nodded. "Okay, you've got it. Just stay out of trouble, okay? Where's the note, because I'm on my way now."

Tearing the bottom from one of her lists, Jeanmarie wrote quickly, folded it small, and marked "Wilfred" on the outside. "Thanks," she said, handing the note to Irene, who tucked it into her skirt pocket and left humming.

For once lights out couldn't come too soon. Already Jeanmarie's eyelids felt too heavy to keep open. She'd come upstairs early intending to get ready for bed when the small torn envelope on her pillow caught her eye. A moment later she thrust it into her sweater pocket. Walking with exaggerated slowness and covering a yawn as she went, she passed close to Pearl and whispered, "Meet me in the john."

As Jeanmarie opened the bathroom door, Pearl slipped in behind her. "What's up?" Pearl asked, turning on the water tap in case someone was listening at the door.

Keeping her voice low, Jeanmarie held out the envelope with the bit of paper in it and read the words "Chicken Thieves." Pearl looked up wide-eyed. "Emma and Leah again. But we didn't take any chickens. I don't get it. They can't know about last night."

"No, or we'd be in trouble by now. They know about the missing key and the missing chickens. Leah overheard Luke tell me to keep mum about the key, so they think they've put two and two together. Those two think we took the chickens!" Jeanmarie rubbed her forehead, which was beginning to ache. "They'll probably try to follow us tomorrow. We'll just have to split up the group. They can't follow all of us once they realize what's happening."

"Great." Pearl sat on the closed john and cradled her chin. "Just when we think things are going better, the bottom drops out. If either one of them decides to snitch it'll ruin everything."

"Maybe," Jeanmarie said. "But they've waited this long, and all we need is a little more time." Now if only Wilfred would come tomorrow. And where was the FBI when you needed them?

In the furnace room of Grant Cottage, Wilfred leaned his thin shoulders against the coal bin wall and looked carefully at the note in his hand. Should he or shouldn't he? Tomorrow he had planned to read that book on Antarctica. On the other hand, Jeanmarie was not one to ignore. The two of them had a quiet understanding. It was Jeanmarie who had discovered his hiding place in the gym storage area the night of the folk dancing. Like him, she didn't feel like dancing. Neither of them had spoken much, just about little things while they waited for the hour to pass. Maybe that was one of the things he liked about her—independence—or was it courage? But getting this pass for a hike meant she probably wanted some kind of favor. He could just not show and think up a reason later, or he could go.

THIRTEEN

A Long-Lost Relative

No!" Jeanmarie cried, staring at Pearl's white face. Across the meadow that ran by the road a carpet of ice-crusted snow glittered with sparkles of sun. It should have been a glorious day, but Jeanmarie felt as if a crack had opened in the bottom of the world, a dark gash. "It just won't be the same without you," she said quietly, turning away to lean on the snow-topped meadow fence post.

"I promise I'll write every week." Tears glistened in Pearl's eyes. "We're still friends and always will be."

Jeanmarie nodded. She couldn't look at Pearl. Any of them could be torn away from the group at the whim of some long-lost relative, only how could it happen to Pearl? What kind of aunt would suddenly show up to claim her niece? It had taken her a good long time to find her. It wasn't fair.

"Listen," Pearl pleaded, "I know neither of us expected my aunt to turn up. I didn't even know I had one. But she has, and there's nothing I can do about it."

Something in Pearl's voice made Jeanmarie turn to her quickly. "I know, and look, I bet she's a peach. She probably had a hard time finding you. Anyway, you're going to be free, and it will be great. No more rules, probably a room of your own." With a show of enthusiasm she took Pearl's arm. "Come on, let's tell the others."

Tess and Maria were standing in front of the snow igloo they had built for the little girls. Tess had just finished adding a small chimney.

"Hey, gang," Jeanmarie called, sounding like a circus barker, "look here, Pearl is going home."

For a moment there was silence. "You mean, home-home, like for real?" Winnie asked.

"She's going January thirty-first. Her aunt is coming for her," Jeanmarie said not looking at Pearl.

"I didn't know you had family," Tess said. "Hey, it's great. I really mean it—great."

Pearl brushed a stray hair from her eyes. "I only just heard about it myself from Dr. Werner. It's legitimate. She really is my aunt, and Dr. Werner says from what he knows I'm bound to like her. She's an artist and sort of famous over in France where she was living up until the war came. She was my father's sister. I guess she's all the family I've got. Real family, I mean."

Maria looked at Pearl then burst into tears. By the time they'd all passed Winnie's tissue box around she was able to talk. "I suppose you won't be coming with us to Gould's this afternoon," she said softly.

"Look, I'm not going until the end of January. Of course I'm coming with you," Pearl said. She took Maria's arm and linked it through her own. "Nothing's going to separate us, any of us, not even my aunt. I'll write and visit. I promise."

Jeanmarie nodded. But she knew nothing would ever be the same again.

"I guess it's sort of like a miracle," Pearl said. Her words sounded hesitant and questioning.

All of them had talked about long-lost relatives turning up, but Jeanmarie had never dreamed that one day it would really happen. She wanted to say something as they walked together to Wheelock Cottage, but the lump in her throat wouldn't go down. Part of her was ready to believe anything, even the faint hope that maybe things wouldn't really work out with the aunt and Pearl would be back.

"Let's just forget that I'm leaving, please?" Pearl pleaded. "I think I don't want to think about it for a while. You know what I mean."

Jeanmarie stood still. Pearl was the one going, but she had no choice; she couldn't stay at the orphanage now. "It's going to be okay, really," Jeanmarie said. "And if you want, we'll forget you're going till you tell us it's time." She turned to the others. "So who said anything about leaving? We'll get the pass this afternoon, and we're off to Gould's just like we planned."

"Thanks," Pearl whispered.

From lunchtime on, Jeanmarie set her mind to willing Wilfred to show up at Dr. Werner's for the passes. She was certain that she was being followed. Whenever she turned quickly there was Leah not far behind. It was almost time to go for the passes. She would have to put plan B in motion. Yawning lazily, she called loudly, "Who wants to play a game of Monopoly?"

On signal Pearl and Winnie settled themselves beside her on the living room floor and began setting up the board. Leah seated herself in the corner of the room by the radio. Maria and Tess stood by the doorway as if deciding what to do.

Jeanmarie lifted her eyes to glance over at the two in the doorway. "Oh well, you two go ahead and do what you have to do. We understand, don't we, gang?" The others nodded, giggling a little as if at a private joke.

"Okay, then," Tess said, her voice just a little loud, "we thought we'd take a little hike, you know. We shouldn't be too long."

"No, it shouldn't take you too long," Jeanmarie added mysteriously. As the girls left, she bent her head over the game watching Leah from the corner of her eye. In a moment Leah was gone.

"I think she fell for it," Winnie whispered. "Should I watch at the window to make sure she follows them?"

"Good idea," Jeanmarie said, continuing to sort out the Monopoly money. "I'll stay here with Pearl in case she comes back to check." She had no sooner finished speaking when Leah, with coat and hat already on, paused to glance into the living room. Apparently satisfied, she left. Moments later the girls saw the tip of her head pass the living room window. As they watched, Leah hurried up the girls' hill after Tess and Maria who were already well on the way.

Jeanmarie grinned. "Let's go. By the time we get our coats they'll be out of sight." There was triumph in her voice. They were down the cellar stairs to the coatroom and into their coats in record time. They still had to get their passes.

Wilfred waved his pass at them as they ran up the steps to Dr. Werner's office. They were almost too late. Coming out of the building Jeanmarie held up her pass for Wilfred to see.

"That was close," he said, coming to stand by the girls. "Do you three always wait till the last minute like that?" His slanting black eyes shone though he didn't smile. Wilfred was usually serious.

"Not if we can help it," Winnie said, tucking her scarf higher against her neck.

"Let's get out of here before we're followed," Jeanmarie ordered. "I'll tell you all about it on the way. We'd better go through the woods by the road, then cross over into the orchard and stick to the orchard till we come to Gould Road."

Wilfred, walking beside them, pushed his wool cap to the back of his thick black hair. "What's all the secrecy about? Who's supposed to be following us anyway?"

Jeanmarie looked at him for a long moment. She began at the beginning and told him everything as they walked. "And today, once Tess and Maria get back, it will be too late for Leah to know where we've gone. Emma is out of the way for a while with her friends from James Cottage."

"That leaves us in the clear," Pearl added.

"Okay," Wilfred said, as if examining the plan Jeanmarie had just explained. "Suppose you've got something here like a black-market ring. If Dr. Werner really is involved in it, how do you plan to make the police believe you? What if they don't find matching packages and can't identify the one you stash?"

"They'll match," Jeanmarie insisted. "We make an anonymous phone call to the police. We give them everything we've got including Luke's accident, which really wasn't an accident. Then we offer to work with them from the inside to trap Werner red-handed." She was sure that sooner or later they would catch Werner.

Wilfred seemed lost in thought. "Hmm," was all he said at first, and then as if he'd decided something he added, "The first part is possible. But I doubt the police will enlist a handful of girls to set a trap for Werner." He was interrupted by a yelping, bounding, yellow-brown dog coming to greet them.

"What are you doing here, old friendly?" Wilfred said, leaning down to pat the dog's head. "He lives somewhere on one of the nearby farms," he explained. "But every once in a while he finds his way over here. Go home, Buster, go on home, boy." The dog sat patiently at Wilfred's feet as if he didn't understand.

"Wait, wait," Jeanmarie said, patting the dog's head. "Nice dog, that's the boy. I think we ought to let him come along, don't you? If the fellow with the dog is still in the cabin he might be helpful." The dog seemed to like the idea and plowed ahead, leaping back through the snow to prance around Wilfred every few minutes.

At the stone entryway to Gould's the dog raced ahead. Jeanmarie stopped with the others to look and listen. Puzzled, the dog ran back to them, pushing his large head against Wilfred's leg.

"I don't think there is anyone here," Wilfred said. "Let's have a look at your cabin." They headed for the cabins away from the frozen lake. They'd reached the cabin and walked around it without seeing anyone. It seemed deserted when suddenly Buster started to bark loudly and ran in the opposite direction.

Jeanmarie felt the skin on her neck freeze. Was it the other dog and the man they'd seen in the cabin? She turned to run and stopped startled, unbelieving at what she was seeing.

A slight distance from the gateposts, heading in their direction, was the unmistakable figure of Chaplain Stone. He waved a gloved hand while he rubbed the head of the dog with the other and continued walking toward them.

There was nothing they could do. "Hi," Jeanmarie said, her cheeks burning.

Chaplain Stone looked at them, his round face showing nothing, not even surprise. "Out for a walk, eh?" he said. "Myself too, and a glorious day for one, eh? I don't suppose you'll mind if I walk along with you?" He paused, but no one made any answer. "Well, good then. Where were you heading?"

"Oh," Jeanmarie heard herself say, "we weren't really sure, just sort of hiking around."

"Right, looking for birds, that kind of thing," Winnie added lamely. Pearl nodded and grinned.

Chaplain Stone patted Winnie's head. "By heaven, child, that's a capital idea; go where the spirit takes you. Now I've a sudden thought; how would you all like to take a tramp in the woods back there by the road to see an owl's nest? Came upon it myself, not an hour ago." Smiling, he picked up a handful of snow, patted it, and tossed it back toward the gate. Buster ran to find it.

Wilfred looked hard at Jeanmarie, tilting his head ever so slightly in the direction of the gate and the woods beyond.

Jeanmarie cleared her throat. "Sure, I guess if everybody else wants to I'm game for the owl's nest." She wanted to tell him no thanks and hoped he'd go away. The others chimed in agreeing to accompany the chaplain. It was possibly the worst afternoon of her life.

The owl's nest turned out to be a deep hole high up in an old tree. Probably the place the owl had come from the other night in the woods, Jeanmarie thought. The rest of the time they spent hiking through the woods they had just left, trying to make conversation. At least Chaplain Stone seemed pleased with their company, and they did manage to keep a steady pace back to the institute grounds.

By 4:00 they were back at the orphanage. "Well now, I'll be leaving your good company," Chaplain Stone said. "But there is one matter I'd like to remind you of before we part. I'm sure you all know that Gould's Camp is a private place. I distinctly saw a 'No Trespassing' sign above the gateposts. Do I need to say more?" A dead silence followed. "I thought not. Now run along and stay away from places you don't belong."

As the chaplain strode away on the road to the boys' hill, Wilfred said, "We're lucky he didn't report us. We could have told him what's going on, I guess. Anyway, it's too late to try again. I've got to be back for supper duty."

Jeanmarie felt too tired to be angry. "If Stone knew, the first person he would tell is Werner. It would ruin everything. We were so close," she said. "We have to try again before it's too late; if they haven't already moved all the evidence."

"Maybe," Pearl mused, "if we use sleds to go down Orchard Hill to Gould's and back to Wheelock the other way, we could go while the Saturday movie is on like we did when we went to the freezer."

"We could do it, and that way we'd steer clear of Stone and anyone trying to follow us." Quickly Jeanmarie explained to Wilfred. "So that way if Maria and Winnie cover for us at the movies, we can do it." She searched Wilfred's face for a sign. "Since there is only one of you, I don't think you'll be missed. Besides, you don't have a Leah or an Emma to worry about."

"Right," Winnie added.

Wilfred patted the dog as if he hadn't heard. "I want to think it over. Anybody hanging out in the camp isn't going to like having us snoop around."

Jeanmarie nodded. "On the other hand, if we bring sleds and somebody is there, they'll think we're just a bunch of kids out for an evening's sledding on the lake."

"That's just dumb enough to be believable," Wilfred said. "If I'm going, I'll cut down from Grant to the orchard and meet you by the foot of the watchtower."

"Swell," Jeanmarie said, turning to go. "And don't forget to bring a flashlight," she called over her shoulder as the three of them walked back to Wheelock.

Glancing down the hill she caught a glimpse of Chaplain Stone rounding the administration building. Funny about him. He didn't turn them in, and he'd acted friendly enough. He had kept them out of the cabin and warned them not to go back. Could he have been following them? Probably not. Most likely they'd just bumped into him on one of his usual walks. Pearl threw a snowball, and Jeanmarie bent to make one of her own. She had almost forgotten. All too soon there wouldn't be any Pearl around. A feeling of heaviness like a hard knot settled itself inside her. She would never read Dickens again.

FOURTEEN

Strangers
in the Dark

*I*n the clear, cold, night air a thousand stars shone above them. Still, Jeanmarie was glad for Tess's flashlight as well as her own. Between them they kept a small steady beam on the path ahead. Behind them Pearl's sled made a soft swishing sound as she pulled it uphill. By now Maria and Winnie were watching the Saturday night movie. If only Wilfred was waiting at the watchtower she would feel easier. She was certain he would be there.

As they neared the tower, Jeanmarie peered anxiously into the dark at its looming black shape. "You there, Wilfred?" she called softly. A slight rustle from the nearest tree brought Wilfred into sight, or rather, almost. He was dressed in a dark jacket and pants and was practically invisible in the shadows.

116

"First we agree on the rules," Wilfred said. "If there is any sign that someone is in one of those cabins or anyplace else when we get there, we back away quietly. After that, one of us calls the police."

"Agreed," Jeanmarie said quickly. The others echoed her.

"Okay, then." Wilfred pulled his sled around. "One of you can ride double with me on my sled," he offered. Pearl volunteered, and in a moment two sleds and their riders were racing down Orchard Hill to the road below.

Braking with her feet, Jeanmarie slowed their sled so that she and Tess hit the opposite side of the road drifts without too much of a jolt. Wilfred's sled careened sideways as it hit a second later, sending Pearl flying into the snowbank.

Brushing snow from her face, Pearl stood up. "Some ride," she commented. Wilfred grinned.

Jeanmarie cupped her flashlight in her mittened hand. "If a car comes, we'd better be ready to dive off this road." The high banks of snow left by the plows would be good cover. "Let's go, gang," she said. "Remember, whatever happens we have to be back when the movie lets out." She glanced at her watch. "Good so far. And when we get to Gould's two of us can go in and two can wait at the gate. There's no sense in all of us walking in, just in case."

The slight incline of the road to Gould's was smooth sledding right to the entryway. Jeanmarie propped Pearl's sled against one of the stone posts. For the next few seconds they stood listening and straining to see what lay ahead. No lights showed, no dog barked. "It looks deserted enough," Jeanmarie said. "Pearl, you and Tess stay here. Wilfred and I will go ahead." She looked at Wilfred.

Wilfred pulled his cap down over his forehead. "Right," he muttered, "only no flashlight. We can see enough without it, and we don't need someone else seeing us." Inside the entryway he took hold of Jeanmarie's arm. "Wait," he whispered. "Let's go 'round back of the cabins. No need to walk in by the front door."

Jeanmarie nodded. "Right." Why hadn't she thought of that the last time? They were at the first cabin. In the silence and darkness it seemed frozen and empty. They crept past it to the next. They were almost to the end cabin. "I don't see any light," Jeanmarie whispered. "And if the dog was around, I think it would have barked by now." She stared at the cabin for signs of life. The only sound her straining ears could hear was the slight crunch of frozen snow under her boots.

Quietly Wilfred moved to stand close beside her. "Okay," he said, keeping his voice low, "where's the window with the chink in it?" The windows facing them were boarded over tightly.

"We have to go around to the other side," Jeanmarie answered. Stepping as carefully as she could, she led the way. The snow crunched lightly underfoot, a worrisome sound. The chink in the boarded window was there, but no light showed anywhere. Jeanmarie held her breath and waited for something to stir. She moved aside for Wilfred to press his face close to the chink. For a long while he stared quietly into the cabin. "Well, what do you think?" she whispered.

Wilfred took his flashlight from his jacket pocket. "I guess there is only one way to find out for sure," he said. Moving her back out of the way, he turned on the light and peered into the window chink. "There's something on the table, a lamp, I think, but the rest of the place looks empty." He moved the light a little, twisting his face flat against the hole to see. "That's it. I can't see much; nothing's there that I can see." He straightened up.

Jeanmarie took his place playing her light first one way and then the other. A sinking feeling gripped her. They were too late. Why hadn't she taken one of the packages as proof the first time? "I think they've taken the packages and left," she said, her voice flat. "But we'd better make sure. Come on, I've got a key that opens the lock."

"This is trespassing," Wilfred mumbled, holding the light as she worked the iron key into the padlock.

"The lock isn't popping like last time," she whispered. "Maybe it's broken." She yanked at the round metal top of the padlock and it parted, surprising her. Gingerly she pushed the door ajar and, holding her breath, stepped inside. Behind her Wilfred swept his light from wall to wall. The cabin was empty except for the oil lamp on the table.

"So where are your packages and your spies?" Wilfred asked, his tone cool and superior.

Jeanmarie walked to the table looking for the book of matches that had been there the last time. "Okay, so you don't believe me," she said. "But if nobody has been here then where are the matches that were here the last time, right next to this lamp?"

"Very good, Fraulein." With a start, Jeanmarie swung round. A man stood framed in the doorway, one hand clamping shut the mouth of a large shepherd dog at his side, the other firmly gripping Wilfred's right arm. "Stay and be quiet," he commanded the dog, releasing his grip on its mouth. A low growl came from deep inside its body, but it stayed at its master's side.

"One word from me," the man said, "and Bruno will tear your throat out. Do you understand?"

"Yes, sir," Wilfred stammered. Jeanmarie could not find her voice, nodding her head vigorously instead. Just as in a bad dream, she wanted to run but couldn't.

"Good. Now you two will come with me. You will not make a sound or move unless I tell you. You will give me your light, please," the stranger said to Wilfred. "Good. Now place your hands on top of your head. Good. You first," he motioned to Jeanmarie, pushing her in front of Wilfred whose arm he still held. "Down the steps and into the woods with you."

Bruno had come to walk by her side, and Jeanmarie could feel his heavy body brushing against her leg. "Please, God, don't let him bite me," she prayed, terrified of missing a step or making a sudden move. She tried to look down without taking her hands off her head. The light from Wilfred's flashlight, held now by the man, showed little in front of her. At the bottom of the steps she started in the direction of the road.

"Halt!" the stranger commanded. "We do not go that way, Fraulein." With his hand on her shoulder he turned her toward the woods in back of the cabin.

Too numb to think, Jeanmarie obeyed. In the weak light of the flashlight she saw what looked like a small path into the woods. It was trampled enough to pack the snow, so it was easy to follow.

"Hey, mister, where are you taking us?" Wilfred cried out. "My father is the chief of police, and when he finds out, you'll be sorry."

It was a bold lie, Jeanmarie thought, but just maybe Wilfred knew what he was doing.

The man chuckled. "So, you poke around deserted campgrounds with your girlfriend while your father the chief of police thinks you are safe at home? I do not think so. Now be quiet."

The man had a point, Jeanmarie thought. Still it might have been true; Wilfred might have a policeman for a father. Like lightning it struck her that Wilfred's real purpose was to let the others hear what was going on, if they were anywhere near, that is. Quickly she called as loudly as she could, "You better let us go, or Wilfred's father will let you . . ." The man's large hand stifled the rest of her words.

Still covering her mouth, his voice low and hard, he said, "One more trick like that, Fraulein, and you will be sorry." He released his hand from her mouth slowly. "Not that anyone can hear you, but you are to be silent. Do you understand?"

Jeanmarie nodded. The man was no fool. By now, she hoped, the girls had run back for help. They had to know that something was wrong. At least he didn't know about Pearl and Tess. Keeping her hands on her head and trying to watch the path was hard work. When another cabin loomed up directly in front of them she dropped her arms without thinking.

"Alright, we go in now," the man said. He knocked on the door three times and it opened, letting out a flood of warm light too deep into the woods to be noticed from the main road. In the doorway another man, shorter and stockier than the first, stood aside for them to enter. Bruno swept his tail from side to side, brushing hard against Jeanmarie's leg as they entered.

"Caught them snooping around the other cabin," their captor said. "This one claims to be the son of the police chief." Still holding Wilfred's shoulder he pushed him forward as he spoke. "The other one has been here before. She knows about the packages."

"So, we have caught ourselves two young spies," the second man said in a tone slightly amused but hard enough to frighten Jeanmarie.

Like the first stranger, he was dressed in dark clothes, his face clean-shaven. As he stood before them Jeanmarie would never have taken him for a criminal she thought, except of course now she knew. A shiver ran down her back. She was beginning to shake from more than the cold.

"Well, Fraulein, what is it you think you know?" the man in front of her asked. "Perhaps if you explain why you are trespassing here we may clear up your misunderstanding," his voice cajoled.

Jeanmarie's thoughts raced, but she was tongue-tied for a moment. "I, we, were ah, exploring, and there were some packages in the other cabin, and ah, we thought maybe somebody was camping out here or something." It was the best she could do.

"Yes," the first man added, "and what was all that about spies from your friend here?" He jerked his head toward Wilfred.

"Oh, well, that was a joke, just a joke," she said lamely.

The second man was looking at his watch. "No more time now for questions and lies. Put them inside, Kurt. Only first we tie them." From under the table he lifted two lengths of rope.

The one called Kurt tied Jeanmarie's hands behind her, did the same to Wilfred, then pushed the two of them through a door she hadn't noticed before.

This cabin had a small additional room, and in it, gagged, tied, and propped against a wall sat the last person Jeanmarie had ever expected to see—Chaplain Stone. His wide-eyed stare was as surprised as hers.

Before she could think, something was stuffed into her mouth cutting off everything but the feeling that she was going to choke or smother. Jeanmarie swallowed and fought the fear that poured over her. Her eyes caught those of Chaplain Stone looking at her above his taped mouth, steadily, calmly, as if he were trying to tell her to hold on.

She could still breathe. The thing in her mouth was just cloth, she told herself as she inhaled deep, slow breaths through her nose. Chaplain Stone nodded his head slightly.

Wilfred too was gagged. For good measure, Kurt tied Wilfred's feet together, then did the same to Jeanmarie's. He patted her on the head when he was through and left her sitting against the wall. As he went out closing the door behind him, thick darkness enveloped the room.

In spite of the dark, Jeanmarie knew the others were there. She forced herself to go on breathing slowly. She wasn't going to smother even though the rag made her want to gag. For long moments she fought the feeling and pushed down the panic trying to rise inside her. She thought she heard a door slam. Maybe the men had gone out. Now what?

If only Pearl and Tess had gone for help. Surely help would come soon. "Dear God, please send someone," she prayed. It comforted her to know that Chaplain Stone was still in the room. She figured he would be praying too. Though how in the world he had gotten here, she couldn't imagine.

At Jeanmarie's side, Wilfred was squirming and making peculiar sounds from behind his gag. Maybe he was trying to tell her something. She wiggled her hands, but the rope was tight. It was the same with the one around her ankles. She stopped struggling and leaned against the wall.

By now Tess and Pearl could be getting help. First she pictured them running to Wheelock and calling the police or maybe stopping a car on the road to ask for help. But what if they had waited at the entryway too long? She pictured the girls standing behind the stone entry posts waiting, wondering what to do, and suddenly being terrified by a huge dog jumping at them. Helpless, she shut her eyes. Like a voice from the past she remembered the Bible verse: "When I am afraid I will put my trust in you, Lord." Silently she repeated it to herself.

FIFTEEN

Betrayed

*T*oo far from the cabins to hear or see what was going on, Tess stood next to Pearl just inside the stone entry posts. "What could be taking them so long?" Pearl whispered. "If they don't hurry we'll all be late." She hunched her thin shoulders against the cold and peered into the darkness.

Impatiently, Tess stamped first one foot, then the other trying to warm them. "I say let's go in at least partway so that we can see the cabin better." It was better than standing still in the cold. They were just about to leave the gateway when Tess thought she saw a flashlight moving near where the cabin should be. "Wait a second," she whispered, "that must be them." Moments later, light showed in the doorway of the cabin again. Then the light turned away from the road and headed toward the back of the cabin. Suddenly

124

Wilfred called out something about the police chief. Some-one else was with them! Pearl gasped. Tess pulled her back behind the stone post quickly. Peering around its corner they saw the light of a flashlight disappearing into the woods just as they heard Jeanmarie cry out. Someone had discovered them!

"We have to follow them," Tess whispered.

"But what if it's the man with the big dog?" Pearl whis-pered back. It was impossible to tell in the dark from this dis-tance what was happening. "I–I think we ought to go for the police," she stammered.

Tess moved lightly into the safety of the bushes along the roadside. Pearl followed her, crouching beside her behind the first tree. They waited, listening for sounds from the camp. Nothing moved; no one came.

"That does it," Pearl whispered. "We've got to go for help fast." Still keeping low to the ground she led the way back through the woods and headed for the orchard road.

"Wait!" Tess said, her voice urgent. "We forgot the sleds!"

"You can't be serious; let them be," Pearl insisted. "What if somebody's found them? It's too dangerous to go back for them."

But Tess was already making her way back toward Gould's.

The darkness settling down on Pearl was too much. "Wait," she cried, hurrying after Tess's retreating figure.

The sleds were still sitting beside the posts. There was no one in sight, and from the entryway the place seemed deserted.

Tess reached for Wilfred's sled. Together they ran back along Gould Road in the direction of the orchard road, the sleds racing behind them. "We have to get the police," Tess said, her breath coming hard. "And that means letting Mrs. Foster in on it, but there isn't anything else we can do."

Gasping and trying not to slow down, Pearl kept pace with her. "Not if we use the phone without Foster knowing and make an anonymous call to the police station," she suggested. "It's worth a try."

The climb up Orchard Hill slowed even Tess to a half-jog, half-walk. Looking back over her shoulder, she called, "Listen, I'm going to steer straight down, across the road, and through into the yard!"

"Okay!" Pearl called back. From the hill any oncoming cars should be clearly visible up either side of the road below. She hoped.

At the top of the hill Tess threw herself face down on the sled and pushed off. Seconds later she swerved sharply into a snowbank. She missed hitting a tree, but her body went twisting off the sled. Behind her Pearl fell in a heap sending Wilfred's empty sled careening down the hill and out of sight.

"What in tarnation are you trying to do? Kill a body?" The thickly clad figure standing in the middle of the road swung his flashlight over the two girls. It was Farmer Banks. His figure had appeared suddenly, directly in the path of Tess's sled.

Between sobs of relief, Pearl stammered out their story. "We've got to get help, Mr. Banks." She accepted his handkerchief and wiped her face.

"Now you think the fellow you saw the other day caught your two friends, eh? Well now, many a time I've run off a tramp or two. As for the dog, there's nothing like a good thick stick." Matching his words to action, he searched for a minute, found the branch he wanted, and broke it off. "Now it 'pears to me that what your friends need most is help right quick. You leave the work to me; just show me where they are. Surprise is on our side."

"Right," Tess said. Farmer Banks was not a small man, and he was strong. "If anything goes wrong, we can still get the police," she said cheerfully.

"Yes, of course. And we will, we will," Farmer Banks promised, "just as soon as we rescue your friends." He walked quickly, and Tess found herself hurrying to keep up. Behind her Pearl was breathing heavily.

At the entryway to Gould's they paused. No light, no sounds. The wind that had blown against them before had died down too. Warm from walking, Pearl loosened her scarf. "Over there in the woods behind the last cabin," she said pointing into the dark. "That's where they are."

"Good," Farmer Banks said. "Now you lead me as close as you can, and I'll take care of the rest." He sounded reassuring.

Carefully, walking as lightly as she could, Tess led the way, stopping at the back of the last cabin. Behind her Pearl crouched low, Farmer Banks beside her.

"Is this it?" he whispered.

In the dark, Pearl breathed a low "Yes."

"Give me your hands," Farmer Banks said reaching for Tess's on one side and Pearl's on the other and drawing the girls to their feet. Without warning his large hands tightened on theirs with a grip of steel.

"You're hurting me," Pearl whispered, trying to pull her hand from his. His grasp on her hand only tightened, crushing her fingers till the pain was almost unbearable.

From the other side Tess struggled to free herself, her voice a loud whisper. "Hey, let go. What are you doing?"

With a vicious yank, Farmer Banks strode through the trees, dragging the girls with him. In a perfectly clear, normal tone of voice he commanded, "Stop struggling and walk. You fool kids, had to stick your nose into everything. Now walk."

Pearl choked back a sob, bewilderment and shock in her voice. "Then you aren't going to help. You never were."

His answer was brief. "This is not a game for children."

Tess too had stopped struggling. In a moment they were pushed up the steps of a cabin. Banks knocked three times at the door, once lightly, twice hard. The door opened.

"I have a present for you, Kurt. Two of them," he said, propelling the girls forward into the room.

The tall man at the door stood aside, his hand tightly clamped on the large shepherd dog next to him. "That makes four of them tonight," he said.

Farmer Banks patted the dog on the head as he passed it. "These are the last. I made certain."

Commanding the dog to stay put, the one called Kurt shut the door and turned to look at the two girls. At a table another man sat drinking from a bottle of cola. A kerosene lamp blazed at one end of the table. Pearl couldn't help noticing the heavy blackout curtains draped across the cabin windows to keep any light from showing outside.

"Well, Wilhelm, it looks like these two are friends of the two in there," Banks said, jerking his head toward a door on his left.

"Kids," the man at the table spat. "We have no time for nosey kids." He reached beneath the table, pulled out two ropes, and handed them to Kurt. "Tie them up and put them with the others. We can question them later," he said.

"Right," Kurt said, struggling with Tess. "Give me a hand, will you, George? Use their scarves for gags; they'll do."

Banks tied Pearl's hands behind her back, stuffed his handkerchief in her mouth, and tied her scarf tightly around her face. She glared at him above the scarf.

When the door to the next room opened, Pearl saw the look of stunned disbelief in Jeanmarie's eyes. As Banks pushed her down next to Jeanmarie, she took in the rest of the group, including Chaplain Stone, all of them tied and gagged like herself.

"Sit," Banks commanded Pearl, though she could hardly do anything else. Kurt propelled Tess to a space on the floor beside her. Like the others their feet too were bound before the men left the room, closing the door behind them.

In the darkness that once more swallowed up the room, Jeanmarie felt something wet slide down her face. Poor Pearl and Tess. But how could she have been so blind about Farmer Banks? That time she'd seen him coming out of Mrs. Gillpin's room, the sinking of the ship right after, even the toothpicks should have warned her. Banks always kept toothpicks in his room in spite of the fact that he had false teeth. She should have remembered the newspaper story Wilfred had read to the class about the toothpicks and invisible ink spies used to write secret messages.

Banks must have caught Pearl and Tess. Nothing was going the way she had planned. Whatever they'd stumbled into, it was serious trouble. Cold seeped beneath the back edge of her jacket and through the floorboards under her. What if nobody came for them? She was the one to blame for getting them all caught. It had all been her dumb plan. At least the FBI had their letter by now. Maybe they were already on the way.

"Please, dear God," she prayed, "please help us. When I am afraid I will put my trust in you, O Lord." Maybe Chaplain Stone was already loosening his ropes. She would never say a word about his sermons again. Maybe she hadn't really paid enough attention in chapel. From now on she would.

SIXTEEN

Surprising Discovery

*T*he Saturday night movie was over. Lights in the gym were already out, and only a trickle of slow movers remained clustered outside the gym door. Maria looked around her for the dozenth time while Winnie pretended to fix the clasp on one of her boots.

"They aren't anywhere in sight," Maria whispered. "We don't dare wait longer." She glanced nervously at the last group of boys heading home. The few girls left were already on the road to the girls' cottages. "Come on," she said.

Letting go of the boot loop that really was frayed, Winnie stood up. "Okay, but now what do we do?" she asked.

"Maybe they went straight home instead of coming here. I didn't see Wilfred with any of the boys. If something held them up and they were late, then they could be waiting for us at Wheelock."

"Maybe so," Winnie grunted, keeping pace with Maria. But it was not so. Trying to appear casual, once inside the cottage, the girls searched all of the possible places the others might have been. There was no trace of them. In half an hour Mrs. Foster would be making her night rounds. What then?

In the living room Emma and Leah were listening to the last minutes of a radio program. The younger girls had already gone upstairs. Leah and Emma usually stayed downstairs until the program was finished.

Maria motioned to Winnie to go upstairs. Tiptoeing to the living room door, she glanced in, then turned in the doorway as if listening to someone. "Me too, Jeanmarie. I'm half-asleep tonight." She yawned loudly. "Just leave my book on the floor by my bed, Tess." She paused for a minute, still standing in the living room doorway. "I heard that, Pearl. Hey, you guys, last one in bed is a rotten potato." With as much scuffling of her shoes as she could manage, she ran up the stairs, taking them two at a time.

In the dorm Winnie was turning down her bed. "Quick," Maria said. "We've got to make the beds look like the others are in them." She ran to the closet, grabbed an armful of clothes, and dumped some of them onto Pearl's and Tess's beds. "Bed rolls," she whispered. "Grab anything you can find and fix Jeanmarie's bed."

Winnie picked up a throw pillow from the foot of her bed and the nightgown she had been about to put on; throwing a box of tissues on top of them, she ran to Jeanmarie's bed. When she was finished, the lumpy form under the covers might have been someone trying to sleep. For good measure she pushed the pillow into a mound, drawing the sheet up to cover most of it. From the doorway it looked as if Jeanmarie was already asleep under the covers, her face to the wall. In Tess's and Pearl's beds the effect was the same.

When Mrs. Foster's arm reached for the light switch just inside the door, a sleepy voice half-buried in blankets called out "Good night." Another groggy voice echoed it. Mrs. Foster turned off the light.

Maria waited until she was sure Mrs. Foster was back in her rooms. Cautiously, she lowered a bare foot to the cold floor. At Winnie's bed she whispered, "Move over, we have to think." Winnie's bed was warm, and the thought of getting dressed and leaving the house made Maria groan. "Something's gone wrong. What if they ran into someone in the cabin? We've got to find out what's happened," she said in a low voice.

"I don't know, but I bet one thing; it's big trouble," Winnie whispered back.

"You don't think that man with the dog has them, do you?" Maria asked.

Winnie frowned in the dark. "If he has, we're the only ones besides Wilfred who know where they are, and Wilfred wasn't back either when we left the gym."

"I know," Maria said. "It was a crazy plan. We never should have let it pass. What are we going to do?"

"Are you thinking what I'm thinking?" Winnie asked. She was already sure of the answer.

"It's the only thing we can do," Maria agreed. "We go see what's keeping them. If they aren't back by 11:00, we'll just have to sneak out." She turned slightly, aware that the edge of the small bed was too close for comfort.

Winnie sniffled. "I don't like it a bit. They should have been back by now. If we're caught, all of us will be on restrictions for a year." She sniffled again. "On the other hand, if anything happened to them, I'd never forgive myself."

The house grew still, and after a while Maria thought she ought to see what time it was. Sleepily, she tiptoed back to her own bed for a flashlight. They must have fallen asleep—it was 11:30, and a quick check showed that the others had not returned.

Down in the cellar the two dressed for the cold. A reluctant Winnie held the flashlight while Maria put on her boots.

When they stepped outside the night wind blew against them. "Let's go by way of the main road through the orchard," Maria said, her head low against the wind. "If they took the sleds they would have gone that way." Winnie nodded.

On the deserted road the going was easier. Maria let her flashlight roam over the snowbanks to her left and right, then back to the road. They were almost halfway up the hill when something sticking out of the snow on the left side of the road caught her eye. "Look, Winnie, there in the snow!" Though a third of it was buried in the bank, what stuck out was unmistakable—a sled. Not far from the first one they found the second one—Wilfred's sled, his name in black across its center bar. "They could have left them here," Winnie said, setting Wilfred's sled upright on its runners.

Maria was about to answer when the startling sound of a motor coming toward them made her jump. "Quick—behind the snowbank!" Leaping over the low bank she fell in a heap face first into snow. Winnie, half-jumping, half-falling, rolled down beside her. The car was stopping. Above them the bright beam of a searchlight moved across the road flooding the snow around them.

"Over there, Officer, over there." Only one voice sounded like that—Dr. Werner's. The light played over their heads like a beacon. Car doors opened and footsteps approached.

"Okay, you, come out of there," a gruff voice commanded.

Winnie stumbled out first, and Maria followed, tripping over Tess's sled. The officer caught her and held her arm to steady her.

Dr. Werner thrust his flashlight close to the sled sticking up in the snowbank. "You are sledding at this hour? First I get a call that we have a runaway on our hands; next I find you two out in the middle of the night. You will explain yourselves," he commanded, his tone stern and cold.

Maria blurted out everything. Winnie added a detail here and there, both girls forgetting for the moment all but the desperate need to find the others.

The officer of the law listened carefully. "Gould's, you say." He looked thoughtful. "It could be," he said, turning to Dr. Werner. "We've had warnings to be on the lookout for anything suspicious, you know. I better radio for help. Meanwhile, you kids will have to come with us."

"You should have come to me right away," Dr. Werner scolded, opening the rear door of the police car. "Why didn't you come to me immediately?" He didn't wait for an answer but climbed into the front seat next to the officer. In the backseat Maria stared at Winnie. It had suddenly occurred to her that Dr. Werner was one of their chief suspects.

They drove without lights. A quarter of a mile from the entrance to Gould's, the officer stopped his car. "This is as far as we go, Dr. Werner," he said. "I want you two kids to stay put in that backseat, hear? If anyone comes this way, you stay down, keep the doors locked, and don't move till another officer comes. Reinforcements should be here soon. You are not to move from here, and that is an order." Opening and shutting the car doors with barely a sound, the men left.

SEVENTEEN

Hard Evidence

*I*nside the cabin, puzzled, Jeanmarie listened to the rhythmic sound of something thick thumping against the wall. Then an idea struck her. Leaning forward she bumped back against the wall, then again and again. In a few minutes the others were adding the noise of their bodies whacking against the walls to hers. She had no idea what it would all lead to.

The door suddenly opened sending streams of light into the small room. It was Kurt. The dog stood beside him. "We do not have time for games. I advise you to be still or you will be sorry." This time he did not close the door behind him all the way. A tiny column of light strayed into the room. At least their thumping had gotten them some light, Jeanmarie thought.

She strained to listen to the men talking in the other room. One of the voices was definitely Farmer Banks's.

"The truck will be here soon," someone said. "Kurt, you check the supply cabin. George, you come with me. Everything must be handled with care. We will start taking out the boxes behind number three."

It was Banks who asked, "What about them?"

The voice of the second speaker was low, but Jeanmarie heard him. "Them? When we finish loading we will deal with them. We cannot have loose ends, nothing must show that we were here."

Jeanmarie shivered. Was she, were all of them, loose ends? A door opened, letting in a rush of cold air. There were footsteps then another voice.

"Better leave the dog here until we come back." Then a door shut. For a minute or two, Jeanmarie could hear the dog scratching at the door. After a while, something pushed against the door to the small room, opening it wider. The men had left the oil lamp on. In the doorway stood the large dog, eyeing her.

Moving slowly, it went over to where Wilfred sat against the wall and began sniffing him. Jeanmarie watched fascinated as the dog started to move its head all around Wilfred's face. It must be licking him, she thought.

Whatever it was that made dogs like Wilfred, it was working. Wilfred turned his head first one way then the other, but the dog didn't go away. Instead, it seemed to be enjoying its game with Wilfred. Tail wagging, it growled and played with the rag tied across Wilfred's mouth. Finally with a jerk the rag caught on the dog's large teeth and tore, leaving Wilfred free to spit out the wad in his mouth.

"Good dog, good dog," he said. The dog worried the bit of rag in his teeth and settled down on the floor to chew it. "Oh, man," Wilfred said, "if I could just get him to bite through these ropes." But the dog seemed intent now on staying where it was.

Wilfred slid himself closer to Jeanmarie. "I think I can loosen your gag," he said, "if you turn your head so's I can get my teeth on it."

Jeanmarie nodded and turned her head away from him. She could feel him trying for a hold on the rag, and once she thought he had it. She bent her head, hoping it would help. Some of her hair was caught, and when he pulled, it hurt, making her jerk her head a little, but it was working. The rag loosened just enough to slip down around her throat, freeing her mouth to spit out the rest. The relief was so great that for a second she didn't speak, just breathed in air.

"Thanks," she whispered. "I thought I'd choke. If only we could find a way to get Chaplain Stone's off," she pleaded, desperately trying to think of a way.

"I can try," Wilfred said, looking uneasily at the chaplain. Two wide strips of wrinkled brown tape crossed his mouth from cheek to cheek. "They must have run out of tape before they gagged us," Wilfred remarked. "I don't want to hurt him." Instantly, Chaplain Stone nodded his head up and down fervently. Wilfred began sliding toward him and Stone toward Wilfred.

Jeanmarie turned her eyes away. In the opposite corner Tess was already working on the scarf around Pearl's face. It finally slipped down. It was longer before Pearl could work Tess's scarf enough to loosen it and pull it from her mouth.

Tess spit on the floor. "Ugh, I think I swallowed threads from that thing."

The sound of ripping tape forced Jeanmarie to turn toward Wilfred and the chaplain. She winced as the tearing sound came again.

Wilfred jerked his head away. "Sorry, Chaplain, sorry."

"It's okay, son," Chaplain Stone said.

"I wish I could bite off some of these ropes," Wilfred muttered, "but I don't think I can."

"No, I don't think you could. In fact, I couldn't do it myself." Chaplain Stone half closed his eyes, then opened them. "We may not have much time before they come back. What are you kids doing here?"

"I guess I'm to blame," Jeanmarie said. "I thought we could lay a trap for Werner."

"Dr. Werner?" Chaplain Stone interrupted. "What's he got to do with it?"

Quickly Jeanmarie filled him in on the details, starting with the first time they had seen Dr. Werner and the stranger the night of the air-raid practice. "So tonight we thought we could take those boxes of chicken for evidence, then call the police."

The chaplain listened quietly till she finished. "It's not all boxes of chicken. Most of it's guns and explosives. Their game is sabotage," he said. "So Werner is mixed up in this too? We've been watching Banks, but Werner seemed clean enough."

Jeanmarie stared at him. "We?" she demanded. "Who's been watching Banks?"

Chaplain Stone gazed at her for a moment. "Keep it under your hat," he said, "but the FBI is in on this. And no, I'm not a real chaplain," he added, "though I think I did a pretty good job of it."

"But the FBI couldn't have gotten our letter before you came. That means they, I mean you, were here all the time." Jeanmarie's face felt hot. "You knew about all this all along."

"We've had rumors and leads but not the hard evidence until now," Stone said. "If I hadn't run straight into Banks with a camera in my hand, photographing evidence, none of us would be in this mess."

Jeanmarie nodded. For some reason she was sorry he wasn't a real chaplain.

As if reading her thoughts, Stone said softly, "We're in a tight spot, but not being a chaplain doesn't mean I'm not praying for help, because I am." He paused for a moment. "We haven't got long to talk; I think I hear a truck coming." The dog had already left the room and was scratching once more at the door. Straining, Jeanmarie listened, but the truck must have stopped, and she could hear nothing.

From her corner Pearl asked in a slightly quivering voice, "Are they going to kill us?"

Stone groaned. "Whatever happens, be brave and pray." He had been working his way up against the wall and now stood on his feet. "There must be something sharp around here to cut these ropes." As he spoke he hopped closer to the outer room.

Jeanmarie pushed her back against the wall and inched her way up until she too was standing and hobbled after Stone. Within minutes all of them were standing and hopping into the other room. The dog, believing it some kind of game, kept bumping into one then another, making progress difficult.

"If I could only get one hand free," Wilfred said, twisting and struggling behind Jeanmarie. "There's a scout's knife in my right pants pocket under this jacket."

"We'll find a way," Stone said. "Without these ropes we'd stand a better chance." On the table the kerosene lamp burned, but there was nothing else anywhere in the room. "It's our only chance," Stone said. "I've got to try and burn off the ropes. All of you get over by the door. Wilfred, you stay and be ready when I reach for that knife." Wilfred nodded.

Jeanmarie gasped as she watched Stone bend low above the table and nudge the lamp with his head. Slowly he moved it near the edge of the table. The glass chimney on the lamp had to be hot, but he didn't stop. A final nudge sent the glass sideways. The exposed flame danced wildly. Stone turned his back to the flame. His lips were pressed tightly together when suddenly he winced and groaned. Jeanmarie felt tears spilling over her face. And then with a mighty effort he was free.

Jeanmarie let out her breath. In seconds Stone had the knife from Wilfred's pocket and cut the ropes from his feet. He was cutting Wilfred's ropes when the dog leaped up against Wilfred, knocking him sideways and sending Stone's arm crashing against the lamp. Flames shot up into the air as kerosene spilled from the overturned lamp.

"Look out!" Jeanmarie yelled. "The curtains are on fire!" In seconds flames leaped toward the ceiling, and she heard herself screaming for help along with the others. The dog barked loudly and scraped his paws against the door. The dry wood of the table and the cabin walls were already bursting into flames. Jeanmarie threw her weight against the door beside Pearl and Tess.

At almost the same time Stone threw open the door and pushed Pearl outside, then Tess. Wilfred tumbled from the steps just as Jeanmarie felt herself lifted in Stone's arms and carried outside. Flames lit up the snow and a terrible heat followed them.

Voices shouted instructions, and she heard feet running, and then arms reached for her. Once again she was carried, this time out of the woods and to the road where police cars waited. Above her someone was saying, "It's okay, Missy, you're safe now. Just take it easy and we'll have you untied in no time."

Flashing lights and shouts were everywhere. The officer holding Jeanmarie sat her gently inside the car. When the ropes were off, he removed his jacket and tucked it over her lap. "There now, you just sit back, and we'll have you out of here in no time."

Pearl and Tess were already sitting in the backseat of the car with coats wrapped around them. Jeanmarie could tell it was them even in the darkened car, but neither said a word. Pearl sniffled and Tess sat silent. Just then someone opened the rear door and put another coat wrapped bundle next to the other two. "That's the lot of you," the officer said. "Next stop is the hospital so we can see to all of you."

"Is that you, Wilfred?" Jeanmarie asked, knowing it was.

"Not now, Jeanmarie," came the reply. It was Wilfred.

EIGHTEEN

The Last Word

At the hospital the last thing Jeanmarie remembered before her eyes closed was the sight of Dr. Werner standing in the doorway with a nurse. Trouble, big trouble, she thought just before she fell asleep.

Morning sunlight streamed through the window of St. Michael's children's ward. For a little while the girls had enjoyed being fussed over by the nurses and given breakfast trays. Then the cheerful floor nurse had announced that Dr. Werner was on his way to take them home. They were in for it now, Jeanmarie thought.

Pearl pushed her breakfast tray aside. "If it hadn't been for Maria and Winnie leading Dr. Werner and the police to us last night, we might not even be here. I mean, we might all be dead." She frowned. "But what do we do now? What

142

about Werner? If he is coming for us that means the police didn't arrest him."

Tess groaned. "Maybe there wasn't any proof that he was part of it, and they just let him go. We could be on restrictions for the rest of our lives."

"Okay, okay," Jeanmarie began, "what we need is a plan."

"Oh, please, not another plan." The voice was Chaplain Stone's. Behind him, pushing his wheelchair, was Dr. Werner.

Jeanmarie stared. How long had they been there? What had Dr. Werner heard?

Stone's arms and hands were bandaged. Some of his hair was burned away, and the burn on his forehead was an angry red.

But he was alive and cheerful. "Well," Stone said, "considering last night's doings, all of you look okay." Dr. Werner pushed the wheelchair closer to the group. "There is one more matter," Stone said, a serious expression on his face, "that needs to be cleared up before we can close this case."

Uh-oh, Jeanmarie thought, here it comes—Dr. Werner.

Dr. Werner looked sternly at her, then at the others. He didn't speak or smile.

"Would you be so good as to enlighten these young ladies, Doctor," Stone said, inclining his head toward Jeanmarie.

Dr. Werner stood straight, his hands resting first on the back of the wheelchair then nervously tapping on its metal frame.

"Yes, well, I understand that you girls are under the impression that I was somehow involved with those saboteurs." He cleared his throat and went on. "Absolutely not. What you thought you saw on the nights you, shall I say, tailed me, was quite the contrary. Gustav Schmidt is an old friend, a butcher who was bringing me sausage, a surprise for my family. A Christmas surprise." He looked hard at Jeanmarie. "Not black market, if that is what you are thinking, hardly that. Gustav had bought deer meat from another friend, deer sausage. He wanted to keep it quiet; a butcher has to be careful in times like these. One could lose good customers if they felt left out."

Dr. Werner's hands had stopped drumming on the wheelchair and now rested on its top. "So, an innocent act, you see, one easily explained and proved, I might add. The second time Gustav came he brought a couple of fine hares for my married daughter's family." As he finished explaining, his hands once more began their tapping.

Stone nodded. "I'm afraid it is all true. Dr. Werner is innocent, and all of you are guilty of a serious accusation." Stone paused, then smiled. "Of course, you are also heroes in a sense. Thanks to you, Banks and his cohorts have been arrested. The whole ring is out of work and will be for a long time to come when Uncle Sam gets through with them." He grinned.

Jeanmarie felt as if a weight had suddenly been lifted from her. "We, I mean, I'm really sorry about thinking you were in it," she said, looking pleadingly at Dr. Werner. "I, we should have known you would never do anything like that. It was just so crazy, I mean, we knew something was going on somewhere. And there were those missing chickens." Her voice seemed small to her, and she stopped.

"Yes, well," Dr. Werner said, "the chickens were Mr. Banks's doing. Now we will say no more of it. Mistakes happen when one jumps to conclusions. However, you have managed to become rather the celebrities, so we shall just have to take the good with the bad." His face softened a little then resumed its straight lines. "Be warned though. I will not tolerate such behavior again. You are not to leave the grounds under any circumstances, and there will have to be some suitable punishment for the worry you have caused Mrs. Foster." He paused as if waiting for an answer.

"Oh yes, sir," Jeanmarie replied. The others chimed in.

"Then I shall sign the necessary papers and return for you in a few minutes." Without further words Dr. Werner left the ward.

"So," Stone said, "that is that. You will probably miss out on the next few Saturday movies, but after this adventure I shouldn't think a few movies will matter."

"Right," Jeanmarie said. "But one thing I can't figure out is what really happened to Luke that time in the watchtower."

"That is easy. Luke probably never did make it up the tower stairs," Stone explained. "Banks must have crept up behind him and struck him shortly before you girls came along. We think Banks was using the tower to signal the men at Gould's. From the tower he could flash coded messages to a man on the road to Gould's. Luke must have arrived early and didn't see Banks. I guess Banks couldn't afford to wait to get his message through."

"Lucky for Banks that Luke didn't see him first," Tess added. "Poor Luke."

"Yes," Winnie pointed out, "but if it hadn't been for Luke's accident we might never have solved the mystery."

Jeanmarie was the last to leave the ward. She lingered behind the others while Stone waited for a nurse to take him back to his room. She wanted to fix this moment in her mind. Even in his wheelchair, though he looked tired now, he was the first FBI agent she had ever met. Besides that he had really been the one who saved their lives. He had risked his safety for them and gotten burned.

"Listen, champ," Stone said as Jeanmarie walked toward the door, "when I get out of here, I'll drop you a line, okay?"

"Okay," she said softly. "I won't ever forget what you did for us last night. You're the real hero." Quickly, without a backward look she ran into the hall where Winnie was already coming to hurry her along.

Back in the orphanage, heroes or not, they were all on a month's restrictions—no Saturday movies, no passes, nothing. Mrs. Foster eyed Jeanmarie warily whenever they met in the hall or dining room. It was as if a cloud of suspicion had permanently attached itself to Jeanmarie, at least in Mrs. Foster's eyes.

Alone in the dorm, Jeanmarie took out the last of her small store of blue notebooks and wrote the word *solved*. She needed to write down the final happenings of the last two days. A slight cough made her look up. Leah was standing in the doorway staring at her.

"I didn't know it was you who gave me that notebook and those things for Christmas," Leah said, surprise showing in her face. "If I'd known it was you, I wouldn't have done all those things. I should have known you never did nothing to hurt me. It wasn't right, the mean things we did, Emma and me." She turned and fled from the room.

For a long while Jeanmarie sat quietly with the blue notebook in her lap. Some things did change after all.

But a lot of things hadn't changed. She still had to work at the farmhouse.

On Monday morning she hung her coat on its peg, straightened her apron, and went up the stairs to the farmhouse kitchen.

From her place at the kitchen stove, Mrs. Koppel lifted her spoon from the pot of boiling cereal and stared hard at her. "This thing with Mr. Banks, this terrible thing is over, ja! Forty years I live in this country, and this is my home. I am an American, and I thank God for America. This Banks deserves whatever punishment he gets." She turned her back to the stove. "You need now and then that I should keep you on your toes, but I think you are pretty smart, ja! You got a good head on your shoulders." With one hand stirring, she waved the other toward Jeanmarie's breakfast. Beside the usual cereal Mrs. Koppel had placed a large sweet roll. She said softly, "So eat it. You deserve a little treat."

In school another surprise waited. A reporter and his photographer had come to interview Dr. Werner about the whole event at Gould's and took a picture of the class. Maybe they would all be in the newspapers.

That afternoon her father called. "You alright?" he asked. "Dr. Werner filled me in on what happened." His voice on the other end of the office phone sounded worried.

"I'm okay really," she said.

"Thank God for that," he said. "Things could have been bad, kid. There's one thing your mom and I agree on. Even if we can't make it together we want you to make it. I'll see you next visiting Sunday; be good, you hear?" Jeanmarie didn't put the phone down right away after the call but stood holding it in her hand thinking. There was something in her father's voice she hadn't heard for a long time. Or maybe she just hadn't been listening. She'd listen better next time he came.

On Sunday there was no chaplain to replace Chaplain, rather, agent Stone. Dr. Werner lectured on keeping the rules. Jeanmarie's starched surplice itched the back of her neck, distracting her just enough so that she heard very little of the sermon. Then she caught the word *fire* and sat up to listen.

"Could have died in that fire," Dr. Werner was saying, "but for the bravery of Mr. Stone, and of course, the help of Almighty God."

Jeanmarie saw again the red tongues of flame leaping in the small cabin. It had all happened so fast. She could have died in that fire, every one of them could have. When they bowed for prayer, she whispered, "Thank you, God." A warm feeling filled her, and she smiled as Pearl's thin hand slid into hers and squeezed tight.

On the following Friday a letter and a package arrived. The package had a Connecticut return address from Mr. Bryan Stone. Jeanmarie tore open the wrapping and took out a book, *Pilgrim's Progress for Young Readers*. On the cover was a boy dressed in old fashioned armor like a knight's and holding a sword. On the inside cover it said: "The uniforms change, but we still fight the same kinds of battles. This was one of my favorite books when I was your age. I'd forgotten until that night in the cabin when things looked pretty bleak for a while that it matters a whole lot whose side we are on, and who's on our side. I hope you'll like the book. And when you're a little older you might consider a more permanent job with the FBI. Let's keep in touch. Sincerely, B. Stone, ex-chaplain."

The letter was from her mom. "They told me about that Gould's thing. Thank God, you're alright." Jeanmarie smiled.

More about This Book

The author spent part of her childhood in an orphanage like the one in *Jeanmarie and the FBI*, and she brings many of her own experiences of life in an orphanage to the story. While Jeanmarie and the others are fictional characters, they represent the children who truly lived in the orphanage.

During World War II there were four Nazi saboteurs who landed from submarines and rafts at Long Island's south shore near Amagansett. Another four landed shortly after at Vedra Beach near Jackson. Boxes of explosives and maps listing targets like bridges, power lines, aluminum plants, reservoirs, and department stores were found buried near the landing sites after the men were arrested. What might have been a two-year campaign of destruction was prevented. The story in the book came from these actual reports of sabotage.

In *Jeanmarie and the FBI* the saboteurs move into Gould's Camp, a place well known to the author as a summer camp for poor children from New York City. The actual Hudson

River spies used O'Brien's Camp, a resort on the Hudson just above New York's 125th Street ferry.

The lowly toothpick used by Farmer Banks was called the Nazi spying tool. One such spy, Kurt Ludwig, an American-born German, told how he picked up hitchhiking soldiers, learned information from them, then used invisible ink and a toothpick to write his reports.

While America fought overseas, the homefront did its part to keep America safe and to help support the war effort. Civilian air-raid wardens, blackouts, rationing, and the collecting of scrap metal were all part of the effort. Unfortunately, there were those people who saw the war as a way to make money by selling rationed goods illegally on what was known as the Black Market, and so Jeanmarie and the others made the mistake of thinking they had run into a black market ring, only to discover in the end that things were far worse. The terrible war brought suffering to many families, but it was a time when Americans of every age came together against enemies that threatened the free world.

Lucille Travis, writer, speaker, and former English teacher, enjoys visiting historic sites and researching old documents. She is the author of several books for children and lives with her husband in St. Paul, Minnesota.

Also Available . . .

APPLE VALLEY
MYSTERIES

0-8010-4470-7
$5.99

In *Jeanmarie and the Runaways*, the orphans learn a real-life social studies lesson. When Jeanmarie finds orphaned migrant kids Juan and Serena, she's determined to help them hide from the evil Don Carlos. But when her plan backfires, Jeanmarie's last hope is telling the truth. The orphans learn the hard way that honesty is *always* the best policy.